Dead

Dead Is Good

By

Jo Perry

Charlie & Rose Investigate: Book 3

Fahrenheit Press

For T., and A., and I., for the dogs and with gratitude to Chris McVeigh who always burns with a fierce, clear light...

"Mictlan is the underworld of the Aztec People…It is a gloomy place, reached by the dead only after wandering for four years beneath the earth, accompanied by a 'soul-companion,' a dog which was customarily cremated with the corpse…"

—Jack Eidt, *"Aztec Myth: Quetzalcotl Rescues Humanity in the Land of the Dead."*

"Unfortunately I am afraid, as always, of going on. For to go on means going from here, means finding me, losing me, vanishing and beginning again, a stranger first, then little by little the same as always, in another place, where I shall say I have always been, of which I shall know nothing, being incapable of seeing, moving, thinking, speaking, but of which little by little, in spite of these handicaps, I shall begin to know something, just enough for it to turn out to be the same place as always, the same which seems made for me and does not want me, which I seem to want and do not want, take your choice, which spews me out or swallows me up, I'll never know, which is perhaps merely the inside of my distant skull where once I wandered, now am fixed, lost for tininess, or straining against the walls, with my head, my hands, my feet, my back, and ever murmuring my old stories, my old story, as if it were the first time."

—Samuel Beckett, *The Unnamable*

1.

"Dying is a universe of its own." —Arlene Ang

Rose circulates through the limitless emptiness—tracing slow, circuitous figure eights in the void above my defunct head.

I should explain that this is the afterlife—and that Rose—a dog with reddish fur too fine to hide her almost skeletal thinness—starved and thirsted to death on the other side.

My name is Charles Stone and I'm dead, too.

I was murdered three years ago—which makes me deceased with a capital D. I have occupied this edgeless territory with the dog since my awkward and—some might say unfortunate—demise.

Here it's No Pain, No Pleasure.

No Air. No Time.

No More Chances.

If You Were Screwed Before, You're Really Fucked Now.

Elevation—none.

Population—two.

Although the dead are immensely portable, we do not often penetrate the impossibly thin and inscrutable margin that separates creatures like me from creatures like you.

We have returned to the world of the living for only two extended stays since my murder.

The first was to find out how and why I died.

Let's just say my murderer was no Dr. Moriarty.

He was a schmuck—an armed bicyclist who lost his temper with an annoying, big-mouth jay-walker—me.

The other time was to help my ex-stepdaughter when she

got in trouble.

There doesn't seem much point in going back—except to give Rose a change of scene.

Or I should say, "a scene."

So Rose and I return now and then to visit patches of living green.

During these brief transmogrifications, Rose pretends to run on or roll in the grass the way a living dog would.

And I take care to avoid the living.

Which isn't hard to do.

On your side we're invisible. Silent. Insensate.

Rose can't feel the tickle of green blades under her dead paws—can't sniff the chlorophyll-infused scent the grass releases under the weight of a living dog.

As she moves—the air does not move through her fur.

Yet she consents graciously to these limitations.

And I suppose I've come to accept my own deadness, too—if not with serenity—then with a certain fatalism.

After some resistance—I'm cool—or I should say—stone cold—with what is.

Which—by the way—is abso-fucking-lutely nothing.

If there are saints or angels, dominions or thrones, seraphim or cherubim—they haven't stopped by.

Ditto for devils, heavenly fathers, sons, sisters, cousins, aunts or uncles—clouds, rainbow bridges, music, white light, tunnels or a welcome committee of the departed.

The Creator?

Don't ask.

Karma?

Otherworldly justice?

If there were justice, Rose's suffering in life would have earned her admittance to a spectral dog park complete with a ghostly hot dog vendor—if there were such a place or entrepreneur in the afterlife.

And there aren't.

There's zip.

Not even one dead and amorous virgin looking for action.

No limitless evergreen field—you know—like that old Microsoft Windows screen saver—below a heavenly blue under which I could skip eternally and blissfully with a gracefully running Rose.

Not that I deserve those things.

I don't.

I don't think I even knew how to skip when I was alive.

I wasn't an athletic guy. Nor was I sporty in any sense of the word.

So why should I start skipping just because I happened to get murdered?

Out of relief to have shed my heavy skin and to no longer be stuck up to my ass in futility with you and the rest of the living on the other side?

Maybe.

It's freakishly peaceful here in the kingdom of the dead.

Unfilled.

Blank.

Vacant.

Idiot-proof.

Clear.

Except for right now—

Rose pauses her meandering motion three feet above my head.

Her dark brown eyes widen, her nostrils flare, her mouth opens as the hair on her neck rises and she barks frantically at something I cannot hear or see.

Then she disappears.

2.

"What to do if you find yourself stuck in a crack in the ground underneath a giant boulder you can't move, with no hope of rescue. Consider how lucky you are that life has been good to you so far. Alternatively, if life hasn't been good to you so far, which given your current circumstances seems more likely, consider how lucky you are that it won't be troubling you much longer." —Douglas Adams

I follow Rose into your fucked-up world.

I could have gone anywhere—to the top of the dome of the Taj Mahal.

Inside Saturn's rings. The tip of Everest.

Tokyo.

Or deep inside the Marianas Trench.

But I hover with Rose just a few inches above the pavement outside the North Hollywood Police Station.

I'd guess it's four or five in the afternoon. The sky is clouded.

Spring? Fall? Winter?

I can't tell.

A small woman jogs right through Rose and then through me—like a piece of paper carried aloft on a gust of wind I cannot feel.

Here there is no me—and there is no Rose—we're permeable.

Imperceptible.

You might say "ethereal," but I wouldn't—"ethereal" is too delicate to ever describe me.

The running woman wears dark, wraparound sunglasses, a navy-blue bandana under a blue Dodgers' baseball cap pulled low on her head, jeans and a white t-shirt with some sort of writing printed on it.

As the woman passes through me, I notice that her freckled arms are the color of milk.

And that she holds a large black handgun in her small pale hands.

Then woman stops running.

She looks back toward the street where she came from— through Rose and through me—as if she's looking for a pursuer—as if someone chased her here.

Then turns her head toward the station entrance.

I see that the small hands that hold the gun tremble.

She takes a breath and holds it, then squints and fires the weapon directly at the glass-block wall at the station entrance.

What the fuck?

Pop. Pop. Pop.

The blocks spiderweb with cracks.

Rose paws the air and replies to the gunshots with a series of sharp warning barks the woman cannot hear.

Before I can stop myself, I rush toward her and reach for the gun. My useless hands melt right through it as the woman fires again.

This time she aims at the top of the glass entrance doors.

Grayish blotches appear as the fortified glass absorbs each bullet.

The gun is still aimed at the doors—the woman looks quickly over shoulder—as if she still expects someone to approach from the street.

Does she have a partner?

What can she possibly think she's doing?

Trying to rob the ATM inside the lobby?

That's insane.

"Drop the weapon! Hands where we can see them!" a deep voice shouts orders from inside the station.

Then the pockmarked doors are kicked open—officers in Kevlar vests and armed with rifles are visible kneeling at either side of the door.

"Drop your gun! Hands in the air!" the voice repeats, louder now.

"Drop your weapon. Hands in the air! Now!" Another voice, this one female. "Or we'll have to shoot you."

But the woman does not drop the gun or raise her small, pale hands.

She resumes firing at the glass door, her expression dreamy, distant.

Jesus.

Did she even hear the officers' warnings?

Is it possible that she is deaf?

Rose yips at the muzzle flashes that spark from the building's entrance—and then at the bullets that explode through the woman's slight torso.

Blood—in wine-colored Rorschach inkblots—blooms across the woman's neck, and arms—covering the words printed on the fabric of her t-shirt.

3.

"Everything that's born has to die, which means our lives are like skyscrapers. The smoke rises at different speeds, but they're all on fire, and we're all trapped." —Jonathan Safran Foer

Pop. Pop. Pop.

Or maybe Bup. Bup. Bup.

You'd think projectiles with such sleekly effective and deadly force would make a more solemn sound as they advance through a living body.

They don't.

The woman's chest and arms receive the bullets unceremoniously—like an old pillow.

Until a bullet enters her forehead.

The shots continue as she folds like a cardboard cutout onto the pavement—the gun still in her right hand.

4.

"What is called a reason for living is also an excellent reason for dying." —Albert Camus

Uniformed officers swarm the woman's body. One man kneels and begins applying compressions to her wounded chest.

The sound of sirens and shouting swirl in the air.

Rose keeps her eyes on the woman, watching her intently as she floats a few feet over her head.

I rise about twenty feet straight up. Fire department paramedics approach from the west on Burbank Boulevard, and a crowd of people—many of them kids with backpacks walking home from the nearby high school—gather on the sidewalk.

Below me there are so many police officers huddled over the woman that all I can see are her gray Converse tennis shoes.

A fire truck's sirens let out a series of loud whoops to clear the driveway.

Once inside the parking lot, paramedics carrying equipment hop from the truck and run to the body on the ground.

The police officers—still in the Kevlar vests—make room for them. A muscular paramedic kneels and removes the woman's bandana and her hat.

The hair that uncoils onto the pavement is like copper and gold spun into impossibly fine and luminous threads—fairytale hair—the kind that attracts trolls.

Then the officer removes her sunglasses.

A shiver of recognition passes through me.

Fuck.
I know her.

5.

"Death is not the worst evil, but rather when we wish to die and cannot." —Sophocles

"One, two, three, four—" A paramedic with bloodied blue latex gloves stops applying compressions to Hope Morgan's chest.

Another lifts her bloodied t-shirt and is about to attach a sensor patch from an AED machine to the skin below her bra when the first paramedic shakes his head.

"There's nothing we can do here."

I move very close to Hope's face.

Her nostrils and eyelids are still.

The bullet hole in her forehead is already darkening, the blood coagulating.

Her lips are turning gray.

The paramedic presses Hope's carotid artery with his finger, then shakes his head. "What time is it?"

A police officer looks at his watch. "Three twenty-two p.m."

The paramedic pulls down Hope's t-shirt.

"I'm pronouncing. Time of death. Three twenty-two p.m."

6.

"Call no man happy before he dies." —Herodotus

A female paramedic covers Hope's body with a sheet.

After a moment Hope rises from the inert form like a person climbing steep stairs from a dark windowless basement into a brightly lighted kitchen.

Rose—her feathery tail swinging back and forth and her head down—sails over to this Hope as if she's greeting an old friend and expects a pat on the head.

Hope ignores her.

"Hope," I say gently.

How long has it been since we spoke? Nine years counting my three years dead.

Hope looks at me.

Her jade green eyes are losing their color. "Charles? Charles fucking Stone?"

I try to smile—I'm not sure if I succeed.

"Why am I surprised?" Hope shakes her diaphanous head and her luminous copper hair, now flecked with blood.

Not the warmest response, but Hope must have lost her equilibrium. Who wouldn't after being shot to death?

No matter what she says—I'm determined to offer Hope—the sister of the only woman I ever loved—and to be completely honest, I still love—a brotherly welcome into death's kingdom.

It's the least—well not the least—it's the only thing someone in my condition can do for someone in hers.

Hope glances down at the covered body—her body—and

observes the officers closing off the parking lot with yellow caution tape. Then she looks at me and frowns.

As I explained before, I'm good and dead—also barefoot and with blood-caked and pewter-colored bullet holes in my shirt and visible in my neck.

"Looks like we both were shot to death," I shrug. "It's a messy way to go—but fast."

Hope ignores me and stares into the group of bystanders gathered at the edge of the parking lot—and then people crowding the sidewalk across the street.

I look where Hope looks.

Young women with strollers, the babies covered with pastel blankets.

A boy on a bicycle.

A white-haired old man walking an old gray dog with a white chin.

A Hispanic man in his twenties in a beat-up white Volvo station wagon stares at the police station entrance and then drives away. A child in a baseball cap sits in the seat next to him.

Hope never liked me.

Never approved of her sister, Grace.

Why should her feelings change just because she and I are dead?

Still, some perversely chivalrous impulse compels me to persist. ""What the hell just happened, Hope? What could possibly make you think you'd survive shooting up a goddamn police station?"

Hope is silent.

"Was this about a boyfriend, Hope? Some fucked-up loser cop boyfriend, Hope?"

It would be just like Hope to date a policeman. Her personality was authoritarian. She loved control, rules and order, athleticism, and competitiveness.

Hope trembles like a kite being tugged skyward on a windy day.

Does she know that she is fading like a flame in sunlight?

That she is migrating elsewhere?

Away from Rose and away from me and into her own dead world?

Now a white L.A. County Coroner's van enters the lot, the light bar on the roof flashing, its siren wailing. A police officer removes the yellow tape and waves it in.

The blue-uniformed driver parks near Hope's body, hops out and opens the back doors.

Hope looks away from the van and seems to notice Rose for the first time.

"What? Now you have a dog? After you're dead?"

"I think the dog has me," I say.

The coroner's people—a woman and a man—cover Hope's body with a dark blue blanket that says, "County Coroner" in white block letters, then lift it onto a gurney and into the back of their truck.

"Come on, Hope. Humor me," I say. "Explain why you felt the need to shoot up a police station."

"I needed to end something. I needed to die," she says. "You gave me the idea to go this way," she says flatly. "Well, not you. Your stupid murder."

Hope is just a glimmer now.

Like a fading, blurring hologram of a beautiful redhead wearing skinny jeans and an unfortunately dark, blood-drenched t-shirt.

"But why?" I ask too loudly and too eagerly—as if my voice could anchor her here. "You were young. Smart. Beautiful. You had everything to live for."

What a stupid thing to say, I think, disgusted with myself for blowing the one chance I have for all eternity to perhaps connect with a person I care about and to understand the horror I've just seen.

"Oh shut up, Charles," Hope's voice admonishes as she thins into nothingness and disappears. "You of all people should understand why—I did it for Grace."

7.

"Everything depends on this: a fathomless sinking into a fathomless nothingness." —Johannes Tauler

Grace.

The sound of her name fills the vacancy that Hope Morgan has become.

Rose whines and tilts her head questioningly at me.

If we were on the other side, I'd give Rose's head a scratch.

But I can't do that here.

I know we'll never see Hope Morgan again, but for Rose's sake I search the air above the police station and the street—though I have no fucking idea where in the vast kingdom of the dead Hope has gone.

After all this time in the afterlife I haven't learned much—except that death is peculiar, conclusive—and private.

Rose's, mine, Hope's—and yours when it comes.

That death surrounds the living—the way dark matter almost fills the universe—eating light—exerting a powerful and clandestine force upon the known.

That only the dead can see the dead.

That each of us is dead—or will be dead—in his or her own way.

That the geography and significance—if there is any—in life's termination is not fixed.

But that doesn't mean that while Rose and I are here in the living world, we can't try to figure out some things—

Why Hope had to die.

And how I can help Grace.

8.

"Death—the last sleep? No, it is the final awakening." —Walter Scott

One of the perks of being dead is attending your own funeral.

For the record—and though I'm not keeping score—Grace Morgan—Hope's sister and the only woman I ever loved—didn't bother to show up at mine.

I didn't think about her absence at the time.

I was freshly dead and my murder had bewildered me.

And I hadn't figured out why Rose was with me—or I should say—why I was with Rose.

Grace was everything to me—once.

The love of my life.

And—yeah—the love of my death.

The love that sat inside me like a stone—changing the way I felt—the way I moved—changing who I was into something else—something better.

If there are more nauseating clichés to describe my love for Grace—and hers for me—I won't offer any more of them to you now.

Just believe me.

She was the one.

And she knew it.

And—as hard as this might be for you to believe—I was the one for her.

Which is why she should have shown up at my funeral—maybe not for the whole goddamn thing—but at least for the graveside send-off and to drop a shovelful of earth on my casket once it had been lowered into the hole.

—
16

Was she still angry?

It would be just like stubborn Grace to cling to a grudge post-mortem.

Why let my murder get in the way of her resentment?

Maybe it's not so surprising that Grace wasn't there.

She hated my family.

Especially my shit brother Mark.

My ex-wives.

My stepchildren.

And our break-up had been final.

Complete and absolute.

More like an amputation than a separation.

After your leg is cut off, you don't visit your dead limb—do you?

No.

You drag your crippled, shuddering damaged self away.

Your lifeless foot doesn't become your goddamn "friend."

Any relationship you had with it is severed.

Kaput.

Your life—like a ripe, fat melon under a Ginsu knife—is split into two scarily neat halves—the time you were bipedal and then when you weren't.

Before.

And after.

When you were whole and when you were broken.

When there was love and when there wasn't.

9.

"Your end, which is endless, is as a snowflake dissolving in the pure air." —Buddhist saying

Grace Morgan.

Seeing Grace again and after everything that's happened makes me feel—what?

Cold—although I am thoroughly incapable of being chilled or warmed.

Still I'd swear over my dead body that a frigid and poisonous mix of dread, sorrow, affection and regret fills the place where my shriveled heart sits inside my ravaged chest—and radiates iciness like an open freezer.

Grace stands barefoot at the end of the Santa Monica Pier—facing the distant smudge that is the horizon.

The tide is high and the heaving gray waves are rough—crashing and hissing at short intervals.

Grace.

Being near her like this—dead and floating close her living form like a comic strip thought-bubble enclosing the words "Watch out, stooopid!"—makes me dizzy.

I close my eyes.

The voices of gulls fighting over flotsam reach the darkness inside my head.

Then I hear what sounds like millions of pins dropping.

I open my eyes as the low clouds split open and release a spatter of heavy silver drops of rain.

The raindrops angle right through Rose as she gracefully zigzags above shorebirds retreating from the foamy waves.

What is Grace thinking?

Why is she standing barefoot there at the edge of the pier in the goddamned rain?

I descend until I'm so close to Grace's dark, curly-haired head that I can see the raindrops catching in her hair—a few new silver strands among the black.

Grace can't know yet that she is alone in the living world.

That her sister—her only living relative—is dead—or how she died.

If she knew—what would she do?

Grace was always quick to anger.

Would she faint?

Become enraged?

Despite the rain, Grace removes her cream-colored rain-spattered cotton jacket, folds it carefully into a square and places it near her feet.

Then—placing both hands on the top metal railing—Grace quickly hoists herself over the railing and jumps into the agitated waves.

10.

"The first breath is the beginning of death." —Thomas Fuller

A man in a windbreaker and a holding fishing pole shouts, "Hey! Did you see? That lady over there jumped!"

Others run to the pier's edge and peer down over the railing:

Two teenaged girls smoking cigarettes and sharing a bent purple umbrella seem unimpressed with Grace's sudden departure into the sea.

A pale flaxen-haired couple in matching green jumpsuits and carrying small black travel umbrellas stare at the empty place on the pier.

A hipster guy in skinny black jeans and a goatee who runs to the railing and then leans over it, taking pictures with his goddamned cell phone.

I sail past the railing and look down at Grace—a hazy, sinking, shape-shifting blob.

Rose abandons the shorebirds and joins me above the place where Grace dropped like a lovely boulder into the sea.

She barks and stares into the waves, then looks at me.

But I can't save Grace.

Can't pull her body up and into the life-affirming air.

All I can do is to sink to the bottom with her.

11.

"Life and death are but phases of the same thing, the reverse and obverse of the same coin. Death is as necessary for man's growth as life itself." —Mahatma Gandhi

A crushed plastic SmartWater bottle, a cardboard tampon package, and I drift six feet below the surface of the mighty Pacific.

Grace is here, too—swaying like squid in the murky water—her eyes closed and—I'd guess—her breath held tight inside her chest.

Jesus.

Is she going to die?

"Grace!" I shout soundlessly. "Stop it! Stop this shit right now!"

But Grace doesn't stop.

She can't hear me and if she could, would she even listen?

She never listened to me when I was alive—about big things like getting married and about small stuff like whether to eat Italian, deli or sushi.

Then the silvered underside of the surface shatters above us like a huge mirror—legs in red swim trunks and the outlines of long, red rescue tubes disrupting the surface.

Lifeguards.

One—African American—with powerful arms and legs dives to Grace, silver bubbles ascending like little balls of mercury from his nose and mouth.

The lifeguard coils one muscled arm around Grace's chest, and with a series of powerful kicks, pulls her up and into the light.

Grace   does   not   oppose   his   efforts—has   she   lost consciousness? Or is she resisting being saved by going limp?

Rose—straight-legged, tense, eyes wide—and I rise with Grace—and watch her head break through sea's choppy surface as she is lifted onto the boat.

12.

"Death is another story. I will never make a joke about death." —Mario Puzo

"You're going to be okay," another lifeguard reassures Grace. "The paramedics are on their way to check you out."

Grace has been dragged from the small boat onto the wet sand, three lifeguards on their knees next to her.

Her dark eyes stare straight up into the rain. Cold convulses her body.

Does she see the people watching from the pier? The crowd gathering behind her rescuers?

That asshole hipster guy with the goatee who was up on the pier is down here now, too.

Now I notice he has neck tattoos.

Jesus.

He's taking more pictures of Grace with his fucking cell phone.

What an asshole.

"Take big breaths. Relax," the lifeguard says.

Grace breathes. Her skin begins to regain its color.

The lifeguards cover her with a silver emergency blanket. The sound of sirens grows louder.

"Can you tell me your name? And how you fell from the pier?"

Grace takes a few more gulps of air and pushes her wet, sandy curls off from her face.

"Grace," she says hoarsely. "Grace Morgan."

Grace swallows more damp, rainy air. "And I didn't fall. I jumped."

13.

"The boundaries between life and death are at best shadowy and vague.

Who shall say where one ends and where the other begins?"
—Edgar Allen Poe

Maybe because I'm in the treacherous, slippery, glittering, moist and—although I can't smell it—perfumed world of the living, I do a really stupid, life-affirming instead of death-acknowledging, thing.

I allow myself to think that if Grace and I had stayed together—she'd be dry on top of the pier right now and I'd be alive and up there with her.

We'd be there taking our three yellow-slickered kids for a crazy rainy-day ride on the Ferris wheel.

Buying them churros and ice cream cones.

Then paying that that weird guy who sits at a card table at the edge of the pier to engrave their names on grains of rice.

What the fuck are their names?

The names of our phantom children are three blanks inside my head.

Three of them?

All boys? Girls? Or a combination?

Shit—did I actually ask myself their names?

I knew I didn't mean those thoughts right as I thought them. They just tumbled into my head and formed themselves into the stalest most dishonest arrangement possible.

But if I had stuck around—isn't there a miniscule chance that Grace would not have felt the need to try to end her life by jumping off the Santa Monica Pier into high tide?

I look at Rose for an answer.

I see a sad, dead, skinny dog—the fur around her neck worn

away—hovering over a woman I haven't seen or spoken to in years who just threw herself off the pier—what James Joyce called "a disappointed bridge"—and into the sea.

Rose looks up from Grace, cocks her head, and stares at me.

Her sweet, sad, wide-eyed, forthright stare is a reproach.

Whom am I kidding?

Churros and ice cream and roller coasters?

Oh fucking really?

I can't fool Rose and—since I died—I haven't been able to fool myself.

Just because Grace and I understood each other—and despite that understanding thoroughly loved each other—doesn't mean that anything would have been different.

I'd be dead and Grace would be what?

Half-drowned?

If love wasn't enough then—why should love be enough now?

14.

"...death, at last is a bore—no more than pulling a shade."
—Charles Bukowski

Okay.

Fuck love.

But I will not fade into the world of the dead with Rose while Grace is like this—alone and in distress and bereft.

So Rose and I stay close—as if we can shield Grace from the beachgoers' nosy stares and although I feel that nothing good will come of our surveillance.

Something is wrong beyond the horrific wrongness of Hope's suicide-by-cop and beyond Grace's senseless dive from the pier—something is dangerously off.

And before something else terrible happens, I need to figure out what the fuck is going on.

15.

"It's a strange world. Some people get rich and others eat shit and die." —Hunter S. Thompson

During the ambulance ride on rain-treacherous streets to the Maimonides Medical Center E.R. in West Hollywood, Grace is quiet but cooperative—not the pain in the ass I loved so much.

I suppose that almost drowning in bone-chilling salt water can make a woman lose her spunk.

Rose stays very close to me above the narrow gurney that supports Grace.

This is not the first time Rose and I have visited this hospital—Rose hates the place.

I died or was pronounced dead here.

We've watched good people suffer here.

And this is where the man who abused Rose used to work.

In the E.R. Grace submits without protest to the nurses who move in and out of the narrow cubicle. Two remove Grace's wet clothes and dress her in two dry hospital gowns, one over the other.

Then they cover her with a sheet and two cotton blankets that they remove from a warmer.

The nurses insert an IV needle into a vein on the outside of her left hand—no wedding ring, I see—take Grace's blood, press a stethoscope against her pale and lovely chest, brush a digital thermometer against her furrowed brow, and wrap a blood-pressure cuff around her arm.

Grace ignores them—studying the fluorescent light fixture on the ceiling as if it were an intricate mandala whose geometry expresses the sacred architecture of the universe.

What Grace doesn't see is me or Rose hanging like extinguished lanterns above her head.

From what I can tell, Grace is fine.

Perfect even.

Her blood pressure is 120 over seventy. Her temperature is ninety-eight point five.

Which means that her attempt to trespass into the world of the dead was a total bust.

16.

"It is worth dying to find out what life is." —T.S. Eliot

Two doctors arrive just as Grace begins to doze. They wear expensive business clothes under their snowy and starched and embroidered white coats.

The man is in his fifties and wears gray wool slacks, shiny black dress shoes and a "cheerful" lime green silk tie.

Already I can't stand him.

The woman—young, pretty, African American—maybe in her late thirties—wears low-heeled black patent leather shoes and a peach-colored cashmere sweater over black wool skirt. A bland pleasantness masks whatever it is she really thinks or feels.

They identify themselves—Dr. Gardener is an internist and the woman. Dr. London—is a psychiatrist.

They offer Grace synchronized bleached smiles, both slightly tilting their smooth foreheads to acknowledge her. Gardener speaks first as if they rehearsed what they were going to say and who would say what before they entered the cubicle.

"Well, you're no worse for wear, Ms. Morgan." Dr. Gardener glances at Grace's chart. "Everything checks out fine. You're a very lucky woman to have survived that fall and immersion in such cold water."

Grace doesn't smile back. And her pupils constrict when she hears the word, "lucky."

"But," Dr. Gardener continues as though Grace had spoken—as if they are having a friendly conversation with

Grace, "Dr. London and I have some concerns."

Dr. Gardener nods at Dr. London.

"How long have you been feeling despondent, Ms. Morgan?"

Grace pulls the thin white cotton blanket up around her neck before she answers. She looks like she's being mummified. "Since you two came in here. How long before I'm discharged? I want to get back to my work."

Dr. Gardener smiles as if Grace just said something really, really nice. "I'm afraid we can't release you until we understand what brought you here, and have completed an assessment of your state of mind today and in recent weeks and months. A suicide attempt is a serious cry for help, Ms. Morgan."

Grace looks away from Dr. London and up at the ceiling again. Rose has begun chasing her feathery tail right above Grace's head.

"I was not and am not despondent." Grace insists.

"But you jumped off the Santa Monica Pier," Dr. Gardener says.

Grace sighs as if she is being forced to explain something obvious to a stupid person, "I told the lifeguard that I jumped. I never said I tried to kill myself."

17.

"It is a curious thing... that every creed promises a paradise which will be absolutely uninhabitable for anyone of civilized taste." —Evelyn Waugh

Grace regards the light fixture as if she were watching the birth of a new galaxy through a giant telescope on a mountaintop in Hawaii on a lucid summer night.

It's really too bad that the living can't see the dead.

If they could—Grace would see Rose—a more lovely and fitting object of contemplation than the light.

And Grace would see me, too—suspended right above her bed, the doctors and the equipment—her personal spectral bodyguard, memento mori and ragged, mortified ex-lover all rolled into one oversized, but convenient package.

Grace's obstinacy and obliqueness don't ruffle Dr. London.

On a scale from mildly annoying to unendurably lunatic— Grace hardly qualifies as spectacularly resistant or even pathologically difficult.

"Ms. Morgan," Dr. London resumes. "Until I'm sure that you won't harm yourself, I cannot discharge you."

Grace lowers her eyes and finally looks at Dr. London. "Okay. I'll admit that what I did was not without risk. But if I had really wanted to hurt myself, I would have jumped from the Vincent Thomas Bridge. In the middle of the night." Grace's voice is flat, her delivery careful.

Dr. London lets her annoyance show. "Then would you explain to me and to Dr. Gardener why you jumped off the pier?"

Grace hugs her lovely knees through the white blanket. "I'm an artist. A performance artist. Do you know what that means?"

Dr. London nods. The other doctor, Gardener doesn't seem sure.

"I used to paint and make sculptures, but I stopped a few years ago," Grace begins. "Now my work involves entering reality and altering it. When I succeed, I change the observer's sense of himself and of the world. People have called what I do 'transgressive,' even 'assaultive.'"

"So you're saying you jumped off the pier into forty-nine-degree water as an art project?" Dr. London says "art project" the way you'd talk about a first-grader's collage.

"Not an 'art project,'" Grace says. "Art."

Rose descends a few feet and slides right through the warm and solid bodies of the two physicians over to the small window. She hovers there and observes the shivering crown of a ficus tree, a wet strip of lawn, and a parking structure.

I know the two physicians can't feel the dead dog percolate through them—but I can't help wondering if their proximity to death hasn't initiated some shivery chemical reaction inside their cells.

Poor Rose—there is no grass and there are no living dogs for her to watch in this gloomy place. Just a man with a red bandana covering his mouth and uselessly waving a leaf blower in the rain six floors down.

Dr. London makes a notation on Grace's chart and waits for Grace to say more. When she doesn't, Dr. London resumes, "What are passersby supposed to learn from watching you risk dying from hypothermia, hypoxia, arrhythmia and ischemia?"

"Each witness takes something personal from the experience I create," Grace says. "I try to shock them out of their ordinary perceptions." Grace closes her eyes, tired from talking.

"There are good surprises, Ms. Morgan, and there are bad ones," Dr. Gardener says disapprovingly.

"I know," Grace says, the defensiveness drained from her voice.

"How do you know?" Dr. London asks. "Have you recently had a bad surprise?"

Grace looks through Rose to the window. "Three years ago the person most important to me was murdered by a stranger. Shot at random on a street in Hollywood. That's when everything changed. When I realized that death is always close. Even when we feel safest and most alive."

Grace looks up at the ceiling again—directly at my dead and damaged heart. "That's what my work is about. I wanted the people on the beach to feel how close death really is."

18.

"I see a dark light." —Victor Hugo

If I had been capable of respiration, my lungs would have involuntarily emptied themselves of air.

If I had been subject to the law of gravity, what Grace said would have knocked me on my ass.

Instead I felt the need to get out of that hospital room and to exit the living world—and to return to the oblivion's pure and silent solitude—to think.

Of course, Rose returned here with me—I go where she goes and she usually sticks with me.

Now, like a fat goldfish—I shift back and forth, back and forth.

I need to think about Grace—and what she said.

Rose seems grateful to be away from the hospital.

She floats serenely on her side below me, head on paws, gentle eyes half-closed and watching me in a feline sort of way.

"'Three years ago,' Grace said."

"An important person was killed."

Rose's eyes widen slightly.

No. "A person important to her."

Or did she say "most important" to her?

I think she said "most."

Rose blinks.

Jesus.

I stop moving—fixed in this vague, unbounded space like the period that follows the last word in the last sentence in a final will and testament.

"Killed in Hollywood." Grace was talking about me—I was that "important person."

I feel like something frozen that's been thrown into a fire.

Rose yawns.

What Grace said changes the meaning of everything—

My life.

My death.

And then—unbidden—a joke my father used to tell intrudes:

A genie appears to a man and invites him to make a wish.

The man thinks for a moment, and then says, "Okay, then. Make me a malted."

So the genie turns the man into a malted.

I'm that still-thirsting metamorphosed man.

I got the one thing I really wanted—the knowledge that I had never lost Grace's love—

Except that I'm deader than disco.

Than four o'clock.

Than Elvis.

Doornails.

Mackerels.

Than my miserable father, Happy Andy the Rodeo Clown.

And God.

19.

"Death is the veil which those who live call life: They sleep, and it is lifted." —Percy Bysshe Shelley

I know what you're thinking——smug and warm and dense with life—that hanging around Grace in the world of the living is masochistic and useless.

That I gain nothing and risk losing the equanimity—sort of—that being three years dead has given me.

And that haunting Grace can't bring anything good to her, either.

That I can't fix what Hope did to herself.

That I can't console Grace or explain a goddamn thing.

Well, too fucking bad.

Now that I've found Grace again I will content myself with mere proximity—with the opportunity to observe—as I am doing now as Grace exits the back seat of a yellow taxi and slams the door shut.

Rose and I osmose through the closed door, watch Grace pay the driver and take a photograph of him—unsmiling out of the driver's side window as per her directions—with her iPhone camera.

The cab driver is a passionate man. He shouted into the speaker of his cell phone in Russian during the way-above-the-speed-limit ride from the hospital to this three-story brick apartment-turned condo building on Fountain Avenue in West Hollywood.

I never visited this place in life.

When Grace and I were together, I had a studio apartment in Hollywood—right off Hollywood Boulevard on

Cahuenga—and she lived in Santa Monica where she had a studio filled with large canvases and wire sculptures.

The morning sky is clear with an almost-transparent and full moon suspended like a bubble in the eastern sky.

A wind I cannot feel scatters shadows of a flowering tree on the sidewalk.

Don't expect me to tell you what time it is.

Someone took my watch and my cell phone when I died.

What I know about the living world I see with my two dead eyes and hear with my two dead ears—thank you very goddamn much.

Grace hands the driver a five-dollar bill as tip.

She is wearing clothes that the hipster from the pier brought to her this morning after Doctor London filled out Grace's discharge papers.

The same asshole who took pictures of her on the pier and then of her gasping on the sand—the twenty-something man with the tattoos on his neck and the fucking goatee.

He carried a Whole Foods plastic bag in which were Grace's black leggings, black boots and a black sweater. The bag also contained Grace's wallet and her cell phone.

Grace called the asshole hipster "John."

While Grace brushed her teeth in the hospital room bathroom, John described himself as Grace's "assistant" to the nurse who had unhooked Grace from her IV. He also mentioned that he worked nights as a bartender in a trendy restaurant in Venice half-owned by the ex-wife of a famous movie actor. Which explains why he didn't drive Grace home and she took this cab.

John also described being Grace's videographer and explained that he filmed all her performances—yesterday's jump from the pier—"Immersion Piece #12." Her "Urban Lost" piece when she lived on Skid Row for three weeks without a coat, cash or a phone. Her "Immersion Piece #10" during which she was lowered into a huge Plexiglas box of venomous snakes.

Jesus.

The last time I saw Grace she was doing self-portraits. Huge angry feminist canvasses that could have been painted by Francis Bacon on acid—nothing like this crazy and dangerous stuff.

I couldn't help noticing that when John talks, the tattoo on his neck moves up and down. The tattoo says, "Life imitates art…" in elaborate, pirate-y navy-blue script, sometimes "Life" reading as "Li fe."

I suspect John's Adam's apple-hugging tat will not look nearly as audacious when he's old and his skin collapses around his throat like a wrinkled sock around a too-thin ankle.

I wonder if Grace has acquired any tattoos during our long estrangement.

I promise myself to check.

20.

"He who does not want to die should not want to live. For life is tendered to us with the proviso of death. Life is the way to this destination." —Seneca

Rose and I pass through the dark wood front door of the second-floor condo as Grace is about to insert her key into the lock.

Shit.

The door is already unlocked.

Grace tentatively touches the door and it swings open. "Oh shit."

The place has been trashed.

Stylized, difficult-to-decipher red and orange spray-painted gang tags cover the appliance-white walls. I can make out a "V" with a heart inside it, a "J", "GL" and "11" spelled out in fat, overlapping letters.

Computers, cameras, printers, and a flat-screen TV sit among the papers scattered on the dark wood floor of the large living room.

Two long tables rest on their sides.

An overturned black leather chair with its bottom ripped out. A gray Ikea style futon couch rests upside down, the mattress cut open, billows of stuffing exposed.

Large bulletin boards have been knocked off the walls.

Black and white photographs, slips of paper, sketches, exhibit announcements and newspaper clippings that hung from the bulletin boards have been pulled off and torn.

One of Grace's huge self-portraits has been ripped from the stretcher bars and sliced into thin strips.

Shards of broken pottery litter on the floor near an

overturned and shattered glass-fronted cabinet.

Burglars would have taken Grace's expensive computers, cameras, video equipment and the flat screen TV, wouldn't they?

This devastation is a message—a threat.

Who would do this to Grace?

An abusive boyfriend?

A stalker?

She stands motionless—her gray eyes darkening as she scans the chaotic scene—her face very pale.

And then she shouts, "Charlie! Charlie!"

21.

"The bitch is dead now." —Ian Fleming

Hearing Grace speak my name—and with such urgency—stuns me.

The longer I'm sequestered in the afterworld, the less real and present I am to myself. I'm even not sure that having a name is practical any longer.

But there is an exception to the-dead-don't-need-names-rule—Rose.

Nameless in life—I felt she deserved a posthumous appellation. "Rose" fits her reddish fur and the feminine softness of her temperament.

Alive I was just Charles.

My parents didn't believe in middle names or nicknames. No Chuck. No Chas. No—God forbid—Chick or Chad.

The only one to address me differently was Grace.

She always called me "Charlie."

"Charlie!" As Grace climbs over the stuff on the floor calling my name, her agitation infects Rose.

Rose swoops around the room like a trapped hummingbird until a dark shape near the ripped futon mattress makes her pause mid-air.

The shape is a hugely fat black and white cat—I think they're called tuxedo cats—round yellow eyes blinking in fear, long white whiskers bristling.

Rose descends until she's close enough to try to sniff the cat's thick black tail.

"Charlie!"

The cat lets out a gurgling howl, then projectile-vomits a lumpy stream of curry-colored liquid in Grace's direction.

22.

"Life is just there, to be made the best of, until it isn't." —
Timothy Hallinan

"Oh Charlie, I've found you," Grace says in a relieved and
singsong voice. She deftly sidesteps the vomit near the
wrecked futon and lifts the cat into a tight embrace. "I thought
someone had hurt you, sweet fat Charlie Boy," she croons. "I
thought someone had taken you away from Gracie."

Rose slides close to Grace—her ears cocked and her chin
lifted—as she watches Grace calm the frightened animal.

Who the fuck would want to steal an overweight dyspeptic
cat? Grace should worry less about cat thieves and more
about whoever broke in and destroyed her condo.

Grace should have called the police the moment she
stepped inside the door.

"Grace!" I shout knowing she can't hear the voice of the
original Charlie. "Whoever did this might be on his way back
right now," I say.

A stern, short series of knocks sound against the surface of
the open front door.

Two uniformed police officers stand in the hallway. One is
a bald, olive-skinned man in his forties. The other is an Asian
woman in her twenties.

"Ms. Morgan?"

"Yes," Grace says, still clutching the cat.

"I'm Officer Ventresca, and this is Officer Ang."

"A neighbor must have called you," Grace says. "As you can
see I've had a pretty bad break-in."

Officer Ventresca exchanges a look with Officer Ang and

then surveys the room. "Yes. I can see that. Please step outside while we make sure your apartment is clear."

Grace moves out of her apartment into the hall, holding the cat in tightly in her arms.

Rose follows her, but I shadow the two officers as they enter the narrow galley kitchen, then the small bathroom, and then Grace's bedroom—all of which have been trashed like the living room and spray painted with the same symbols—a heart inside a "V", "J", "GL" and "11."

The police officers return to the living room and wave Grace back inside.

"The apartment is clear. Whoever did this is gone. We're going to call in another unit to handle the break-in. But I need to explain to you that we're here about something else."

Grace is confused.

"We've come about your sister, Hope Morgan," Officer Ventresca explains.

"Hope? What happened? Is she hurt?" Grace asks.

"Miss Morgan," Officer Ang says. "I'm very sorry to have to tell you this, but your sister was involved in a shooting yesterday afternoon. I'm afraid that she lost her life."

"What? You're saying Hope is dead?" Dazed, Grace wobbles, but stays upright, and loosens her grip on the cat.

Officer Ang nods and takes Grace's arm to steady her. "We're very sorry for your loss."

"A shooting? Where?"

"North Hollywood," Officer Ventresca says. "Your sister approached the police station with a weapon and opened fire at the station entrance."

"But why?" Grace asks, shaking now, as if she's very cold.

"We were hoping you could help explain that to us," Officer Ang says.

"It can't be Hope. Are you sure?"

"We're reasonably sure, Ms. Morgan," Officer Ang says gently. "But as next of kin, only you can provide a positive I.D. We're here to drive you to the Medical Examiner's office."

Grace gently shoos the black and white cat into the bedroom and shuts the door. For a moment she stares at the broken pottery on the hall floor, tears making her eyes shine.

"Before we go, I must ask you to please take a look around to see if anything was taken during the break-in." Officer Ventresca says.

Grace robotically complies with the police officer's request—opening and shutting kitchen cupboards, lifting up piles of papers, checking the contents of overturned drawers.

"Nothing was taken. Heirlooms were broken, but there's nothing stolen," Grace finally says.

Officer Ang nods, "Thank you, Ms. Morgan. Are you ready? Are there any family members you'd like to call?"

"I'm ready. And no. There's only me."

Officers Ang, Ventresca and Grace walk out into the hallway. Rose and I are right above Grace's head.

As Ventresca walks to the building exit, he speaks into his police radio, "Requesting an additional unit at two-two-one-three-seven Fountain Avenue, West Hollywood for a four-five-nine investigation. Gordo Locos tags on the walls. Officer Ang and I will be transporting the resident to the Medical Examiner for a victim I.D. Her sister was involved in that four-four-four in North Hollywood this afternoon. I think the ADW with firearm and this four-five-nine might be connected."

23.

"Life is eternal; and love is immortal; and death is only a horizon…" —Rossiter W. Raymond

Officer Ventresca guides the black and white SUV off the 5 Freeway and onto North Mission Road, then into a short driveway past a modern sign illuminating the Los Angeles Coroner and Medical Examiner's crests and the motto, "Law and Science Serving the Community."

He drives past an ornate ripe-red brick and concrete building to the back near a modern, beige building, and parks below "DEPARTMENT OF CORONER ADMINISTRATION OPERATIONS" painted in black block letters on the beige stucco wall.

Was I taken here after the hospital declared me dead?

Officer Ang opens the police car door for Grace and they lead her across the lot and up the steps of the main building, then over the black and white mosaic that says, "LOS ANGELES CENTRAL HOSPITAL," past the gold-painted windows—"County of Los Angeles / Department of / Medical Examiner-Coroner / Business Hours / Monday-Friday / 8:00A.M.-5:00P.M. / (323) 343-0512 / Emergency / (323) 343-0714," in English on one window, Spanish on the other—into the lobby.

Rose and I move through the gold paint on the glass—then through the blinds and into a marble-walled space.

On the left is a dark wood and glassed-enclosed information booth. A pretty young African-American receptionist wearing a purple shirt nods at Officer Ventresca and slides a small adhesive visitor pass through a slot.

Officer Ang hands it to Grace and she peels it off the paper and sticks it on her sweater.

This is not what I expected.

The place where the murdered, the mysterious, the anonymous and indigent dead are housed should be hell of a lot more noir—and creepy. But except for the sign that says, "Please be considerate of our families here on business," this could be the lobby of any old office building filled with accountants, lawyers and orthodontists.

The walls are marble. The doors—all closed—have mottled-windows with a white feather design. Formal, black-outlined gold painted words—Identifications, Notifications, Property, Gift Shop—decorate the doors.

The quiet is profound. Some unseen force mutes and absorbs each sound before it can reach anyone sitting on the Mission style red leather and wood couches arranged near the wide staircase on a wine and blue oriental style rug.

Even the people are soundless.

A round gray-haired woman in velour pants and a sweatshirt weeps silently. A huge man with a ponytail sits next to her and holds both her hands.

A box of white tissues—one tissue pulled up like a plume of cumulus—sits on the coffee table between razor-straight fanned arrangements of *People*, *Redbook*, and *Family Circle*.

Did my shit brother Mark have to wait on this couch staring at a box of Kleenex?

Did he have to schlep all the way down here from his house in Benedict Canyon—or the office in west L.A.—to pick up my wallet and my watch and tell somebody behind one of these glass doors that the dead fat man was really me?

Did he have to park, walk in here, get a parking pass and a visitor sticker from the receptionist, and then go back to his car to display the permit—all while his extremely important afternoon was being pissed away?

I fucking hope so.

And at three in the afternoon on a Friday when traffic is hell.

Then I remember the hospital I.D. bracelet I still wear on my arm.

They took me to the hospital—not here.

And the hospital is only a fifteen-minute drive for Mark from his house in Benedict Canyon—if you know which canyon roads to take.

And Mark knows. He's too busy and much too important to be stuck in traffic with a bunch of slow-moving schmucks driving Camrys.

Rose hovers above Grace like a butterfly as the officers guide her over the gray, black and white mosaic floor and then wait near the door marked "Identifications."

I don't want to think about where dead animals like Rose must go.

To clear my head, I drift to the door painted with the words, "Gift Shop." A note taped to the door says, "Closed for Lunch—11:30 to Noon."

I melt through the note and the glass behind it—Rose watches me but stays with Grace.

A black leather couch fashioned from a coffin sits under a window ledge displaying model skeletons. Merchandise printed with the store's logo—the black outline of a prone dead body—fills the shelves:

Thermal lunch bags.

Mugs. Baseball hats.

Cutting boards.

Duffle bags.

Stickers. Pens.

Beach towels.

A barbecue apron says, "L.A. Coroner Medical Examiner Has <3,"and on the pockets, "Spare hands," "Spare Ribs."

Beanie animal toys.

Lapel pins.

Polos, t-shirts and hoodies.

Little glass things labeled "suncatchers."

Beige plastic skeleton-arm and toe-tag key chains.

Even a stuffed animal—"Freddy, The Forensic Bear."

48

Above the cash register are two signs:

"Shoplifters' Next-Of-Kin will be Notified." "Checks Accepted with two forms of I.D. or Dental Records."

Real fucking comedians these coroners and medical examiners and death investigators must be. Very goddamn clever.

I know souvenirs. That's part of what my family's business, AndyCo., sells—Happy Andy apparel and tchotchkes—but nothing like this chazerai.

Maybe it's a good thing my shit brother didn't come down here.

If he had, AndyCo.—and its hideous parent company—MultiCorps—would be producing—on the ultra-cheap of course in Mexico—and making even more money than they already are—destined-for-landfills Happy Andy suncatchers and cutting boards right now.

24.

"The dead are everywhere." —Thomas Lynch

Rose's bark alerts me that something has changed.

She hears things I can't—and she knows things that I do not understand.

I melt through the Gift Shop door and see that Grace follow Officer Ang and Officer Ventresca through the door marked "Notifications." Rose and I drift inside behind them past a row of cubicles and to a small office.

Grace sits in the one wooden chair, and places both her hands flat on the Formica desk as if to steady herself. The police officers stand behind her and Rose and I float over their heads.

From behind a modern desk cluttered with files, a middle-aged woman wearing a red sweater under a Coroner's Office black windbreaker speaks to Grace: "I'm Miss Spring, Ms. Morgan. You have been asked here to identify the remains of a decedent who may be your next of kin. The decedent is here because state law requires the Department of the Medical Examiner-Coroner to inquire into and determine the circumstances, manner and cause of all sudden, violent or unusual deaths, and deaths where the decedent has not been seen by a physician twenty days prior to death."

Ms. Spring pauses to let what she's said sink in.

Only after Grace nods does she resume, "For identification purposes, I am going to show you a photograph of the decedent's face. If from that photograph you can make a positive I.D., then I will ask you to sign Form Five."

Grace nods once, inhaling—and then keeps the air inside her chest. Her nostrils widen a little with the effort.

Ms. Spring opens a file folder that sits on the top of a pile of folders and removes an 8½ by 11 color close-up photograph of Hope's face. In the picture Hope's copper hair has been pushed back and a gunshot wound—dark and grayish around the edges and coagulated in the center—sits like a blind third eye in the center of her forehead.

Grayish spatter discolors the pale skin on one side of the wound.

Hope's eyes are closed.

It's not clear where Hope was when the photo was taken, but there is something white under her head.

Grace looks at the picture and gasps.

Officer Ang pats her arm.

"Oh God. It is. It is Hope."

Grace begins to cry. She covers her face with her hands and her shoulders slump.

Ms. Spring slides the photo back into the file and pushes a printed paper, a pen and a box of tissues toward Grace—then waits. I assume that the paper is Form Five and that there is a similar pause and pushing of a tissue box almost every time Ms. Spring shows someone a picture of their deceased next of kin.

Grace uncovers her face, takes a tissue, dabs her eyes, and shakily signs the form.

Ms. Spring slips the form into the file folder that holds the photograph of Hope. "A physician here in the Medical Examiner-Coroner's office will examine the decedent and determine the cause of death. A death certificate will be issued only after this examination is completed."

"What about Hope's things? Her clothes? Her purse?" Grace asks.

Which makes me wonder about the gun.

That's another item to add to my list of Things To Do While I'm In The Living World.

"Any of the decedent's personal possessions currently in the custody of the Department of Medical Examiner-Coroner may be claimed by the legal next of kin. That's you. However, governmental documents—driver's licenses, passports, military identification cards—will be returned to the issuing agency for disposition, in this case, the Los Angeles Police Department. If you have any questions you may go to the Personal Property section on the first floor where a the personal property clerk will advise you if any documents will be needed to claim the decedent's possessions."

Grace nods again, "When can I get Hope out of here?"

"When you select a funeral home, please inform the funeral director that the decedent's death is being handled by the Department of Medical Examiner-Coroner. Ask them to please notify us that they will be handling the arrangements. Our department will need a written authorization to release the deceased, signed by you as the legal next of kin. I am very sorry for your loss."

Ms. Spring stands to signal that the meeting is over. Then Grace stands, too.

But when Grace reaches the office door, she stops. "I can't leave without seeing my sister," Grace says. "I need to see her now."

25.

"The hills are shadows, and they flow
From form to form, and nothing stands…" —Alfred
Tennyson

"I'm afraid that's impossible, Ms. Morgan," Miss Spring says.
"We do not allow viewings here at our facility."

"I have to be with my sister."

"If you will wait in the lobby," Ms. Spring looks at Officer
Ventresca, then speaks into the silent air, "I'll see if I can
locate the handling investigator or an examiner. I can't
promise anything. This is a very busy place."

26.

"A good name is better than fine perfume, and the day of death better than the day of birth." —Ecclesiastes 7:1

Officers Ang and Ventresca follow Grace back into the absolutely silent lobby.

The old hand-holding couple is gone.

Grace stands near the curving staircase.

The unnerving quiet is thick and weighted—almost deafening.

A middle-aged man in blue scrubs good-looking enough to be mistaken for a television actor enters the lobby from a narrow elevator area behind the staircase. He carries a slim file folder. His rubber-soled clogs make no sound as they travel across the antique mosaic floor. "Ms. Morgan?" the man asks and extends his hand. "I'm Dr. Flassman."

"Can I see my sister now?" Grace asks.

Was Grace always so abrasive?

Yes she was.

Dr. Flassman—high-ranking and official representative of this charnel house—is friendly but unyielding, "I'm afraid that's not possible, Ms. Morgan. For reasons of health, safety and privacy, we do not and cannot offer viewings of the deceased at this facility. But I'd be happy to answer any questions you have."

"Okay," Grace says, accepting defeat, "tell me exactly how my sister died."

"The autopsy has not yet been completed—and we don't have toxicology or other lab reports yet. So there is nothing I can tell you officially about Ms. Morgan's death. However, I will say that I suspect nine-millimeter rounds penetrated a lobe in your sister's left lung, her diaphragm and her forebrain."

"Okay," Grace says, "I know she was shot, but—"

Dr. Flassman looks quickly at Officer Ventresca, then back at Grace. "I went over the police report. Emergency responders did their best, but your sister's injuries were catastrophic. For reasons or delusions unknowable to me, but perhaps known to you, your sister actively sought an armed confrontation with police officers, then failed to comply with their commands and escalated her attack against them. I'm sorry to have to say this," Dr. Flassman speaks gently now, "but your sister died because she wanted to."

27.

"Love of life is born of the awareness of death, of the dread of it." —Ian Fleming

While Officers Ang and Ventresca wait for Grace near the restrooms, they inspect the contents of a glass display case mounted on the wall—black and white photographs of the building when it was a hospital and faded group pictures of nurses wearing long white dresses and elaborate caps.

"I kept thinking about those tags in Grace Morgan's condo," Officer Ventresca says. "When I worked Central, I saw tags like those—the Gordo Locos."

Officer Ang looks surprised. "The GLs? Are you sure? What possible link could Grace Morgan have to a downtown gang?

"I have no idea—maybe coke?" Ventresca says, "But my gut tells me that the connection is Hope Morgan."

28.

"Land and sea, weakness and decline are great separators, but death is the great divorcer for ever." —John Keats

Grace sleeps.

The fat black and white cat—Charlie—dozes next to her shoulder in the large, white bed while Rose hovers over both of them—her intelligent eyes calm and alert—as if she's waiting for something or someone.

What?

I'm above Grace, too—a wavering shadow—contemplating what Hope did—and trying to figure out why Grace's apartment was vandalized.

Why did Hope die?

For Grace.

What did she mean?

Because of Grace?

Or for Grace?

Instead of her?

On her behalf.

It has to be that—

Hope said that I—forlorn in-life and in-death lover—would understand.

That the person who loved Grace would understand.

So Hope must be where all this shit begins.

Grace murmurs something in her sleep—it sounds like "No, stupid."

The cat sighs.

Rose blinks.

Did Hope do something terrible? Irrevocable?

That doesn't sound like the Hope I knew.

Soon after Grace and I broke up, Hope left L.A. to attend U.C. Santa Cruz. I heard later on that she studied law at Boalt Hall at Berkeley.

Until I saw her get shot I thought she was still in northern California practicing law.

That made sense—Hope was always practical, deliberate, and orderly.

She grew up with their father—a C.P.A.—far from turbulent Grace and the chaotic life she shared with their artist mother.

You might have heard of her—Judy Morganthal.

In the seventies and eighties she was known for her ceramic bowls and vases glazed with images of ample pink-and-brown-fleshed naked women fucking—fucking men, fucking women, fucking vegetables, fucking fish, flowers, exotic animals and birds. Judy's work had a childlike and sexualized color-saturated, earth mother matriarchal, lesbian vibe when that vibe was fresh and new.

A few years after Hope was born, Judy elevated her consciousness, dumped the CPA and her job as an elementary school art teacher, and moved to Topanga with a man she met at the Renaissance Faire. Grace told me his name was Ricardo—a drummer, biker and a beeswax candle-maker from San Anselmo.

Judy's cluttered ceramics studio and the sprawling house in Topanga Canyon, was—before her death in 1989 from uterine cancer—a place where artists and students, feminists, environmentalists, actors, comics, folk singers and hippies and poets hung out.

Grace had newspaper articles about Judy and her work. She kept them in a special acid-free box on a shelf in her studio, each yellowing sheet separated from the other by delicate semi-transparent pieces of embossed rice paper: "Morganthal's Feminist Vessels"; "Liberating Ceramics" and "Judy Morganthal's Voluptuous Women." "Judy Morganthal's Canyon Salon."

Grace and Hope were as different as Rose Red and Rose White in the fairytale.

One was dark and strong—the other willowy and moon-pale.

One steady—the other mercurial.

I've forgotten exactly how the Rose Red and Rose White story ends—except that a dwarf and a hungry bear are involved.

So how can the ending have been any good at all?

29.

"Men fear death, as if unquestionably the greatest evil, and yet no man knows that it may not be the greatest good." — William Mitford

An empty recycled cardboard cup from L.A. JUCE sits on the floor near the head of Grace's bed.

Rose—her back and front legs straight out—her thin form midway between the ceiling and Grace—focuses her always-open eyes on Grace's closed eyelids.

Neck-tattooed—and I noticed because he was wearing a tight short-sleeved Arcade Fire t-shirt—completely and grotesquely arm-tattooed assistant John brought the juice and a lentil sandwich—whatever the fuck that is—for Grace before he went to work at the restaurant.

That was how many hours ago?

The condo is quiet and dark except for a dull bluish light seeping in through the closed blinds—perhaps moonlight or a streetlamp.

Or maybe it is the faint radiance stars emit as they die.

Did I mention that a police officer stands guard in the hallway—another shaved-headed buff guy in his mid-twenties named Officer Tedford.

Which must mean that the police have no idea who has it in for Grace.

Did I tell you that while Grace was at the morgue, the cops dusted the place for fingerprints and removed a few pieces of broken pottery?

Then—after Officers Ang and Ventresca brought her back here—they helped Grace right the futon and asked to sit and answer a few questions.

When was the last time you saw your sister?

Six years ago.

Where was that?

At our father's funeral.

When did you last speak to your sister?

At the funeral.

Six years is a long time. Were you estranged?

I guess you could say that. Yes.

Do you know anyone who is angry enough to trash your condo?

No.

To destroy your dishes?

Those weren't dishes. They were my late mother's ceramics.

An ex-boyfriend perhaps?

Who knew that they meant something to you?

No. No boyfriend.

A former girlfriend, then?

No.

A business partner?

No.

Do you use recreational drugs?

No. I drink, but I don't do drugs. I don't like the way drugs make me feel.

How about your sister? Was she a user?

Hope? Are you kidding? Hope was too uptight to ever do anything illegal.

Do you know anyone or have you worked with anyone involved in a violent crime?

Yes. I did. A very close friend was murdered three years ago. But they caught the guy who did it. It was a road rage incident.

This friend's name?

Charles Stone.

Getting back to your sister—can you tell us what caused your estrangement?

We were never close. We didn't grow up together. Hope lived with our father and I lived with our mother. We were completely different. To be honest, we didn't agree on much of anything.

What about your assistant? What can you tell us about him?

His name is John Pierce. He's been my assistant for two and a half years. He works nights as a bartender at the Slate and Thistle in Venice. Have you heard of it? The food is organic. They have their own farm in Oxnard. The bar is supposed to be a huge scene.

Officer Ang took notes on a small pad. So did Officer Ventresca.

Did your sister have a boyfriend?

I don't know.

Did she ever have a boyfriend to your knowledge?

Yes. When she lived up north she was engaged to a guy she met in law school. But they broke up.

Do you know why they broke up?

No. But it might have been politics. Hope became more radical in her thinking after she did some pro-bono work after law school. I think Alan just wanted to settle down and make a lot of money doing entertainment law.

What kind of pro-bono work? Any work with gangs?

I'm not sure. Evictions, immigration—that kind of stuff, I think.

Alan's last name?

Alan Bardman. I think he works in Beverly Hills.

Your sister's wallet and clothing were checked, but there was no note. Any reason you know of why your sister would want to kill herself?

Grace snores now—a languid, regular, attractive snore that I recognize with joy. I know her snore's starts and pauses by heart—the way you know a poem you were forced to memorize in school—

Blah. Blah. Blah.

I was about to say that hearing that snore and being close to Grace this way makes me ache—that my need to touch Grace is so powerful that I hurt.

But I couldn't ache if I tried.

Still—I feel a raw and insistent longing—which must be

what pain feels like to a phantom limb.

What could be wrong with easing that pain by sharing Grace's bed while she's asleep?

Would the chill proximity to death shock her awake?

She spent the afternoon at the morgue and look—she's sleeping just fine.

Rose watches me—one ear cocked skeptically—as I lower my big, lucent, deceased body close to the cat and to Grace's opaque, tangible, oxygenated, warm and living form.

Then—like a captive orca performing a trick—I turn on my side and slowly descend until my face is very near the back of Grace's head.

Now I wait.

30.

"If I lived a billion years more, in my body or yours, there's not a single experience on Earth that could ever be as good as being dead. Nothing." —Dr. Dianne Morrissey, a near-death experiencer

A powerful and pleasurable disturbance should be rumbling through me right about now—just as it did every time when—alive—I touched Grace or was close to her.

Nothing.

Not even a tiny flutter of unrest.

Yet I remain where I am—my altitude and position calibrated exactly so—close—and yes, I'll say it—to my beloved.

I concentrate all of whatever I am into effecting some sort of exchange of whatever I've become with what Grace is.

I close my eyes and summon the memory of the coconutty smell of the lotion Grace used on her feet every morning and every night.

The heat of her skin against my skin.

The powdery smoothness and the long taut muscles of her thighs.

Her sharp, rough elbows.

In my mind's eye I see Grace's sweat-damp hair resting in tendrils against her long neck.

Her dark eyelashes against her cheekbones, her worried eyebrows relaxed into straight lines.

Grace stops snoring, mumbles and turns toward the emptiness that is me.

Does she discern somehow that I am right here with her?

I cannot fight the grateful compulsion to kiss the back of Grace's head or to move my fingers through the confused ringlets of her hair.

Before I can stop myself—I move my fingers toward her curls.

But I feel no silk. No fire.

I open my eyes and see my numb dead hand slide right through Grace's hard and living head.

31.

"Death takes place because cell division is not everlasting but finite." —August Weissman

Rose and I have returned to the Medical Examiner's office.

This was Rose's idea.

But it's a relief to be away from Grace and her bed—and the grotesque way she makes me feel.

Rose glides above the driveway, but doesn't enter the old main building or seem to want to revisit quaint lobby. Instead she drifts through the darkness—it's the middle of thc night—toward the new building in back.

The visitors' parking spaces are empty, but white coroner's vehicles, an ambulance and two police cars are parked near the entrance.

I follow Rose as she floats purposefully above the concrete ramp into the modern building, melts through the closed wide doors and into a fluorescent-lighted corridor.

Rose moves down the corridor, her eyes moving from closed door to closed door.

A young woman with honey-colored skin and long magenta hair in a braid pushes a gurney along the pale blue striped linoleum floor and around a corner. The small hands steering the gurney wear tight blue latex gloves. I see the Coroner's Office Crest on the sleeve of her navy-blue uniform as she passes us.

A blue plastic cover marked with "Los Angeles County Coroner's Office" in white letters softens the outlines of the human body resting on the gurney.

"Hey, Sabrina," an African-American man wearing the same

uniform says as he walks by, "what's new?"

"Same old," the girl says as she pushes the gurney down the hall and then stops to press a button that slides open a steel and windowed door.

Rose follows the girl, pausing near her magenta head as she opens a door and pushes the gurney into an anteroom filled with equipment.

The girl pushes the gurney to another door, taps a button, and waits until this door slides open.

Cloth-under-plastic-wrapped corpses are stacked on stainless steel shelves ten high along one wall, and in rows, heads in, the bare dead feet exposed.

Some of the bodies have crumpled brown paper bags resting on top of them.

Along the other wall are more metal carts and a jumble of stainless steel equipment.

Rose watches the girl—Sabrina—as she unzips the blue plastic coroner's bag to reveal the body inside, pull out an empty metal shelf, slide the body onto it, and shove the slot back toward the wall.

Is this room a cooler?

It must be very cold in here. Glacial.

And the too-still air must hold the stink of decomposition.

But the girl with magenta hair seems comfortable, at ease— untroubled.

Rose's paws are relaxed as she lifts her eyes from the girl and directs a meaningful look at me.

What?

What now?

What does Rose want me to see?

I look around the room again and watch the girl push the empty gurney out the door, and then watch the door slide shut.

Now Rose and I are alone with the extremely quiet and introverted people on the shelves.

It's a regular fucking necropolis in here.

And Rose keeps staring at me.

Giving me that look.

I scan the room again, trying to figure out what Rose wants me to notice.

The stiffs look very stiff.

Their feet protrude from the tightly-bound-with-string-at-the-ankles white cloth and or plastic that encloses them. The feet are a grayish pink—or gray—and brown—some of the big toes wear blue or red plastic tags.

Am I supposed to read the goddamn tags?

DERBY, ALLEN.

TIFF, BERNARD.

MARVID, RITA.

PHATI, ANKOUSH.

BALL, JUSTIN.

SANCHEZ, JAIME.

ARVIN, KIRBY.

SHIRLEY, JULIA.

SORRENTO, BARBARA.

JONES, D'EARVIN.

Last name. First name. Then the year and a dash and four more numbers embossed on the shiny surfaces of the embossed, plastic tags.

What does a red tag mean?

I drift close to a red tag attached to an old and battered foot: JOHN DOE.

Does Rose expect me look for Hope?

Is that what this is about?

What would be the point?

Rose knows that Hope is gone.

I float up to the very top shelf.

The dead below me appear strangely compressed.

Like packages of meat beyond their Sell By dates in a supermarket back room awaiting transport.

It's not that they don't look human—they do.

Here and there I see a brightly painted toenail—indicating vigor or joie de vivre before the fatal catastrophe arrived.

But now these people have been muted and simplified.

—

I read somewhere that during autopsies they remove and weigh the organs.

Then what?

Do they stuff the organs back inside or throw them away?

I float to the body at the far end of the top shelf.

Rose drifts near to me as I look closely at its slender form, the shape of its small head visible under the plastic.

A child?

I look at Rose.

Rose floats past the small corpse to a body resting on a lower shelf, pauses, then points her nose toward it, then repeats the maneuver, sailing from one body to the next, then back to me.

What the hell?

I look at the bodies again.

And then I think maybe I get it—

Rose wants me to see the whole dismal fucking picture—all the dead at once—packaged and arranged on shelves like—what?

Bags of crap.

No—not crap—something less than and more neutral than that.

They're just nothing.

And so are we, Rose and I.

I'm not Grace's lover—I am one of them.

32.

"...unless a kernel of wheat falls into the earth and dies, it remains only a single seed. But if it dies, it produces many seeds." —John 12:24

Rose and I levitate a few feet away from the fat boy.

A street lamp about half a block away illuminates his dark baseball cap, baggy blue jean shorts, knee-high white socks, white tennis shoes and a plain white t-shirt.

He shakes a can of spray paint until the metal ball inside loosens and rattles, then depresses the button and points the nozzle at the battered metal shutters that protect one of a series of small closed shops that line the narrow downtown Los Angeles street called La Moda Street.

Later the storefronts will open to the sidewalks—spilling racks and piles of shoes, shirts, dresses, hats, belts produced here in the fashion district—toward the crowds of shoppers.

But now all is quiet and shuttered and in pre-dawn shadow. He must have lots of time before school begins to deface the whole fucking neighborhood.

I guess from the smear of light in the eastern sky and from the time we left the morgue that it's a little past 6:00 a.m.

The boy steps on an empty plastic milk crate and spray-paints the top of the shutter with a large red circle, takes off his cap to scratch his head, then steps down to the littered sidewalk and into a honey-colored beam of morning sunlight.

Rose doesn't like the paint can's hiss and darts a few feet behind me.

There's no point hanging around. I pivot in the air toward Rose.

Wait.

The light makes the boy's shiny, shaved head gleam and reveals the contours of muscular shoulders. His forearms are heavily tattooed.

He is a dwarf—not a child.

A man.

The dwarf steps back up on the crate, lifts the paint can, fills the center of the circle with a fat "GL" and a stylized "7".

Below the circle he sprays—in exaggeratedly angular letters—"Victor."

I came downtown looking for gang signs that resemble the ones in Grace's apartment. After listening to the cop, I figured that "GL" must stand for Gordo Locos—Fat Crazies—and that the Gordo Locos operated near the LAPD Central Division on East Sixth Street.

Besides being fat and crazy, the Gordo Locos must be a powerful gang. As Rose and I wafted through the streets, I could see that most of the area in and around the Fashion district is Gordo Loco territory.

Fat red and orange GL's like the ones in Grace's condo mark stop signs, light posts, walls, sidewalks, dumpsters and doorways.

The dwarf has moved a few doors down and is painting another GL in a circle on the glass window of a taqueria. Then "Victor" again and the "7."

Perhaps he is claiming victory over a rival gang?

Or maybe his name is Victor. The seven I don't get at all.

But what connection could this guy or the Gordo Locos really have to Grace or to Hope?

Maybe it's John.

Is it possible that Grace would piss off a gang as a performance piece?

Maybe.

Pissing people off is one of Grace's talents.

But why would that push Hope to kill herself?

Grace didn't mention gangs when she spoke to the police officers about her work. And if she'd known the Gordo Locos, she'd have said something, wouldn't she?

Would she protect the people who trashed her condo and destroyed her mother's ceramics?

No.

The connection to the Gordo Locos can't be Grace.

That police officer was right—it has to be Hope.

33.

"Death is the penalty that all must pay for the crime of living." —Charles W. Chesnutt

I need to find out what Hope was doing.

But I have no fucking idea where she lived or worked.

Rose and I could drop in on Hope's ex-boyfriend—the entertainment lawyer—and look around his office for her address. But didn't Grace say that they hadn't been dating for years?

And visiting this Bardman guy would violate my strict Never-Go-To-Beverly-Fucking-Hills—The-Place-On-Earth-I-Hate-The-Goddamn-Most policy.

I could return to Grace.

But after our little jaunt to the morgue I get the feeling that Rose thinks that moping around Grace is a shitty idea.

And right now Grace is safe.

She's got that cop posted outside her condo and the hipster assistant.

So Rose and I have returned to the only place I know for sure that Hope Morgan recently occupied—the place where she chose to die in the most public and efficient way.

34.

"Death is the golden key that opens the palace of eternity."
—John Milton

Hope wanted to make sure that everyone—or someone in particular—would know that she was dead.

Who besides Grace?

And why here?

Did someone pursue her here?

But there's no place safer than a police station. So why did she choose to die?

Why pick the North Hollywood police station as the place where she would transit from the living world into that place that comes next?

"Don't Be A Victim," a sign outside the police station entrance admonishes.

The public parking spaces beyond the sign are empty. Maybe it's too early in the day for complaints or visits to the ATM inside.

Past the public entrance area a row of gleaming police cars is angled toward the large windowless extension of the building in the back.

Rose and I glide above the still-shattered glass entry, then dissolve through the plywood covering the damaged glass block wall and into a modern lobby with a curved counter—also made of glass blocks—was there a sale?

An attractive female officer with blond hair stands behind the counter and talks into a telephone. The name on her badge is "Mendez." "A lost ferret, sir? I'm sorry to inform you that it's illegal to own a ferret in the state of California. A senior ferret? I understand. But I'm afraid here is nothing our department can do. Have you tried posting an ad on Craigslist? Or calling Ferret Rescue?"

There are two closed doors off the lobby. One behind the reception area and Officer Mendez—the other must lead to the back of the station.

Door number one or door or number two?

Rose floats over Officer Mendez's head to the heavy black door.

I follow Rose through the door and into the large, fluorescent-lighted space that must be the roll-call room.

A podium and a dry erase board on wheels stand in the front. Rows of black folding chairs and those beige tables they sell at Costco are arranged in neat rows facing the podium.

There is a bulletin board on the wall and a hot water urn, plastic baskets of instant coffee, creamer and tea and insulated cups.

No doughnuts.

I drift toward the board and scan the papers posted in a neat grid.

"REMINDER: Contact your Watch Commander about Deployment Period Days Off—Do Not Email requests for schedule changes.

LAPD Police Family Fun Day and Celebrity Golf Tournament—Volunteers needed—Contact PO 1 Officer Mendez.

Annual Memorial Relay Race. 1-mile fun run, a platoon run, 5K and 25K runs, memorial ceremony, and award presentations. The day begins at 0815 hours. Interested participants or attendees should contact the Los Angeles Police Revolver and Athletic Club's Athletic Department at 323-555-5222 and ask for extension 555.

Blood Drive. Dare To Keep Kids Off Drugs. Retirement Party.

East Valley Police Activities League (PALS) Meeting—First Wednesday of each month.

Police Cadet Post Meeting—Every Tuesday 6:15 p.m.-8:15

p.m.

Last warning!—FOUND Boots—On top of Lockers. Size 12."

Rose hovers behind my shoulders until I've finished, then floats—with me right behind her—into an open office filled with computers, file cabinets, and a large TV screen on the wall with map of Los Angeles with the major streets and freeways lit up in red, green and blue.

Uniformed officers come and go, answer phones, work computers, and write reports with pencils in longhand.

Why don't they use computers?

A dispatcher wearing earphones sits at a desk facing three computers and other equipment.

I don't see Officers Ang or Ventresca.

I move to any place I see paper—and look for Hope's name. Rose and I drift to the back and through an equipment room.

Then a locker room.

I am about to turn back and find the sergeant's office when Rose sails right through the metal lockers and then through the vomit-green cinderblock wall.

I follow her and pass through the cinderblocks to the other side—where a long metal bench is attached to the wall.

An overweight, sunburned, shirtless man in filth-stiffened dungarees sits on the bench. The handcuff on his very pink wrist is connected to the wall with a short metal chain.

He sits very still and his eyes are closed. I'm not sure if he's asleep, awake or passed out.

Rose floats close to the handcuffed man, her tail between her legs, then turns to me with an anxious look.

I shrug. "I think he's okay, Rosie," I say, but she remains tense and growls when a male uniformed officer approaches carrying a plastic bottle of water. "Thirsty Goldberg?"

Goldberg opens his eyes. His pupils are a rheumy, pale gray. Jesus.

And I thought I looked bad.

The man called Goldberg nods. The officer hands him the

plastic bottle and Rose watches him as he drinks it all at once.

Because Rose lived her life hungry, thirsty and tethered—she hates restraints and chains.

But she relaxes a little as she watches Goldberg drink.

"Thanks," Goldberg says and hands the officer the empty plastic bottle.

"You've got to break your habit of defecating in public, Goldberg," the officer says. The name on his badge is Morales. He is muscular and tall, with a pronounced bluish shadow beard darkening his jaw.

"That's easy for you to say," Goldberg says. "I just can't help myself."

"They'll be transporting you to Van Nuys in about an hour, Mr. G," Morales says. There is no sarcasm or cruelty in his voice. "You'll get a toilet, bed, a couple of hot meals, a shower and a clean jumpsuit. Maybe ask if you can see a doctor."

"An ass doctor or a shrink?" Goldberg asks.

"I don't know. How about both?" Morales says. "I'll be down the hall. If you feel the sudden need to take a crap, whistle."

Goldberg nods and reseals his eyes with sunburned lids.

So they don't keep anyone that they arrest here.

Did Hope know that?

I wonder if she died here because she wanted to send a message to someone she thought must be inside.

Someone in jail?

Or an officer?

"Rose," I say, wishing I could pat her head, "I'd like to go into the other room."

I nod in the direction of the office area—and after a long look at the lost, fecally incontinent and dehydrated Mr. Goldberg—she follows

35.

"Dear, beauteous death, the jewel of the just! Shining nowhere but in the dark…" —Henry Vaughan

I want to make one more circuit around the office—to see if maybe Ang and Ventresca have arrived—and to check if there's anything I've missed.

Rose accompanies me as I hover over desk after desk—glancing at page after page of paper and scanning computer screens.

I find nothing that concerns Hope.

Rose stays close as I pass through another black door and into the sergeant's office.

A bald man with a huge black moustache sits at a desk covered with papers. I move behind him and look over his shoulder.

Arrayed in front of him are what must be work schedules for the month to come.

Under those papers corners of other reports are visible—but the disembodied cannot lift a sheet of paper, cannot open a drawer, cannot switch on a computer or type on a keyboard.

This is useless—I'm useless—I decide and float toward the door.

That's when I see it.

A tall file black cabinet to the left of the door.

On it sits a metal Out box with a stack of papers on the top shelf.

There's a burglary report—and underneath it the top corner of another document is visible—boxes filled in with handwritten words and numbers—"Name: Morgan, Hope.

Address: 1442—"

The word that follows the street number is partly obscured—all I can see is "Palo."

36.

"Life ends with a snap of small bones, a head cracked from its stem, and a spirit unmoored…" —Sam Kernochan

Rose traverses the green space—floating through the long purpling shadows broadcast by the big house and toward the huge stand of bamboo to the east—skimming the tips of the respirating blades of grass—until she reaches the otherworldly cacti and succulent garden and then glides back toward me.

It's been an hour or two since the massive wrought-iron gate on Orlando Road was closed and locked, and since the last cars slowly exited the eucalyptus-shaded Huntington Library and Gardens parking lot.

I needed to clear my head and think.

And Rose needed—and deserved—some open space—at least for a little while.

I thought Rose might like this place—the smooth and massive lawns on either side of what is now a gallery and was once where Arabella and Henry Huntington lived with their collection of rare books, paintings, and silver and gold tchotchkes.

I watch Rose sail up and over the bronze statue of Diana and her stag at the foot of the library steps, and then return to the place where I linger near the custard-colored residence's tall and ornate portico.

For a moment I consider going inside the library.

I'd have the treasures to myself—the Ellesmere manuscript of *The Canterbury Tales*, the Guttenberg *Bible*, Audubon's massive *Birds of America*—Shelley's notebook, Lincoln's letters—

But I can't stop thinking about Hope—and what Palo means. Tree?

Palos Verdes.

Palomar.

Pallor.

Palomino.

Palombo.

Paloma.

Palo Blanco.

Fuck.

On what Palo-blank-blank street did Hope live?

I'm getting nowhere.

Rose turns and drifts past the library roof and then over a small forest of tree-high camellias.

I rise into the air that turns cobalt with the coming of evening—and follow Rose.

Over a weathered statue of Triton, then above a large conservatory roof and children's garden westward to a grove of citrus trees heavy with unpicked fruit—and beyond that to a domed structure on a little hill.

Rose dips in and around the columns edging the circular monument.

Now that I'm close I see what it is—a small, domed Greek temple—all gray-veined marble—with gently tapering Ionic columns.

I drift inside and see—not sculptures—but a large sepulcher—the sides of which are carved with softly draped figures with downcast eyes—one with huge feathery wings— and incised with quotations—

SO-TEACH-US-TO-NUMBER-OUR-DAYS-SO-WE-MAY-APPLY-OUR-HEARTS-TO-WISDOM—PSALMS XC12

HEAVEN-LIES-ABOUT-US-IN-OUR-INFANCY— WORDSWORTH

EVERY-SHEPHERD-TELLS-HIS-TALE-UNDER-THE-HAWTHORN-IN-THE-DALE—MILTON

I float around to the front:

IN MEMORIAM
HENRY EDWARDS HUNTINGTON
BORN AT ONEONTA N.Y.
FEBRUARY TWENTY-SEVENTH EIGHTEEN
HUNDRED AND FIFTY
DIED AT PHILADELPHIA PENNSYLVANIA
MAY TWENTY-THIRD NINETEEN HUNDRED
AND TWENTY-SEVEN
and ARABELLA DUVAL HUNTINGTON HIS WIFE
BORN AT UNION SPRINGS ALABAMA
JUNE FIRST EIGHTEEN HUNDRED AND FIFTY
DIED AT NEW YORK N.Y.
SEPTEMBER SIXTEENTH NINETEEN HUNDRED
AND TWENTY-FOUR

This tomb—open to what I imagine to be heavily citrus-scented air—is the real and permanent Huntington residence—not that other house full floor to ceiling with tall paintings and over-wrought French furniture.

Rose rises to the top of the dome and looks down at me.

As always her big brown eyes pose questions I cannot answer—mysteries I cannot solve.

Why do we suffer?

How—exactly—do we apply our long-dead hearts to wisdom?

And what exactly is a fucking dale?

A vale?

A valley?

Then another question occurs to me—

Why did Hope choose to die in North Hollywood? In the Valley? Why that police station and not different one?

Rose's slow descent leaves her right above the stone sarcophagus. She remains above it—as motionless as the dead married couple inside—as still as the figures disturbing its smooth mineral surface.

Wait—

How did Hope get there on the day she died?

If she drove herself to North Hollywood—what happened

to her car?

The police officers never mentioned a car when they spoke to Grace.

And if Hope didn't drive—did someone drive her there? Did she take a taxi?

Did she walk?

Or did she use public transportation?

The Metro station is only a few blocks away from the police station.

37.

"The day after Paul Newman was dead, he was twice as dead." —Maurice Sendak

Rose and I slip through the bright orange canopy in the center of the small plaza—then pass through the warm bodies that belong to people riding the down escalator into the underground—until we reach the mezzanine of the North Hollywood subway station.

It's after rush hour.

Only a few people step past the kiosk and down to the track level where they stand staring into their cell phones.

Many ignore the TAP card machine on the wall—so much for honor.

I look around to find a map of the Metro system and see one near the ticket machine.

Rose comes with me, then hovers philosophically as I study the diagram.

The L.A. subway system is pretty straightforward.

There are two blue lines—one light blue, one dark blue—a purple line, a red line, a green line and a gold line.

The Yellow Line curves from Pasadena through Union Station to east L.A. The Blue Line runs from Culver City through South Central L.A.

The Red Line runs to the valley from Union Station downtown.

If Palo-something Street is downtown—or if she began her final journey in Gordo Locos territory—Hope could have taken the Red line all the way to North Hollywood—it's the end of the line.

38.

"Death is terrifying because it is so ordinary." —Susan Cheever

Welcome to Pershing Square
  For the Safety of Everyone
NO ACLOHOLIC BEVERAGES DOGS MUT BE ON LEASH NO CAMPING / LODGING NO BICYCLES NO SKATING NO OPEN FIRES NO LITTERING NO AMPLIFIED SOUND NO TRESPASSING IN FOUNTAIN NO BICYCLES NO SKATING NO OPEN FIRES NO LITTERING NO SHOPPING CARTS NO BLOCKING PASSAGEWAYS NO SOLICITATION/VENDING DOG DEFECATION MUST BE REMOVED BY OWNER PARK HOURS: 5:00 AM—10:30 PM—NO LOITERING.
  Rose loiters over a flock of pigeons fighting over corn chips some litterer has wantonly spilled and failed to remove from the ground.
  Rose and I travel above the once palm-treed and elegant and now just fucking hopeless concrete Pershing Square in downtown Los Angeles, AKA the land of NO.
  Living human beings without alcoholic beverages, without leashed or defecating dogs, without campfires or bicycles, skates, fires, litter, or amplified sounds—without homes or pots in which to piss—have arranged themselves horizontally along low barriers and next to the metal trash receptacles and on the ground.
  I presume they sleep—unless dreaming is prohibited too— here in this bleak mostly paved pasture with its statue of

Beethoven.

Its futuristic Metro station entrance.

Its Doughboy memorial.

Its silent iron cannon.

The squat processed-cheese-yellow snack bar.

The purple fountain with its narrow waterfall.

The orange concrete spheres that are supposed to mean something or honor someone or fill the desolation.

We move away from the Square and I look around—the jewelry district over there—the Biltmore. The Omni.

Up at the high rises.

I'm lost—and Rose must be lost, too—because she is with me.

I used up my time in the living world in the Valley. Then in Hollywood. Or on the west side.

Not here—I was never the kind of guy who worked in a bank downtown.

The AndyCo. world-fucking-headquarters where I toiled is in a low-slung building near Inglewood.

I wish I could forget about the mystery of Hope's death and the location of Palo Whatever Street and return to Grace.

But I set my dead gaze in the direction of La Moda Street and the Gordo Locos and move.

39.

"...that which is called death hath now come. ...Do not cling, in fondness and weakness, to this life." —The Tibetan Book of the Dead

It's been night for a long time when Rose and I finally locate the battered sign indicating Palo Pinto Street.

It's not a street at all—just a short stretch of alley joining two narrow curving one-way blocks between La Moda Street and the back of the L.A. Trade Tech campus.

1442 is a dirty metal door on this narrow alley lined with windowless, dirty metal doors. To the side of one of the door is a battered mail slot. Above it someone used a black marker to inscribe the street number in shaky and downward-sloping numerals.

The alley looks industrial—as if the spaces behind the doors are places used to store or manufacture things—not places where people live.

Did the cop writing the report on Hope make an error copying her address from her drivers' license?

If she had one—so far I've heard nothing that tells me that Hope owned a car.

Security lights above the doorways throw sickly beams onto the ground, upon the No Parking At Any Time signs, and across the stucco walls between the garages or storage areas or whatever these places are.

Red Gordo Locos spray-painted tags mark the walls, the padlocked Dumpsters, and are the only embellishments in this so-empty-it-feels-lunar place.

I ascend a few feet and peer into the dark windows of 1422's second floor.

No light glows behind the blinds—or travels through the dusty, pockmarked pane.

Rose joins me halfway between the ground and the roof.

If it is possible for darkness to reflect darkness—that's what Rose's eyes do now.

The deep pure gloom of her eyes is a reprimand.

Do I have any fucking idea what I am doing?

40.

"I just put my feet in the air and move them around." —
Fred Astaire

Our world is the afterlife.

Not this one.

But we are here for ever-lost Hope.

For Grace.

Rose blinks.

I do not bother saying these things aloud to Rose—I have
no reason to believe this—but I expect that she knows—
generally—what I feel and think—and why.

Or if she doesn't than she might as well.

We descend together almost to the ground—and pass
through 1442's metal door into a shadowy, low-ceilinged
warehouse.

The security light outside sends thin bands of greenish light
across a scuffed black and beige linoleum floor.

I wait for my dead eyes to adjust to the darkness—but they
don't.

Rose moves across the room—a smudge of darkness inside
the dimness—then stops mid-air and whines softly.

I float to the back wall where Rose hovers.

Beneath her in the dark are three dark shapes—one large,
the others small—rest on a quilt or on an open sleeping bag.

Rose whines again and moves close to the smallest shape.

I follow.

In the jumble of shadows I see a woman with long, dark hair
sleeping on her side—a small toddler pressed against her
chest—and a child that looks like a boy asleep on his back.

I sink through the dimness until their soft and regular breaths are audible.

As if he knows I'm here—but he can't—the small child on his back moans and kicks off the blanket.

He wears only one sock, a disposable diaper and a too-big white t-shirt with writing on it.

Rose makes a thin, high-pitched sound I've heard her make when she sees a living puppy.

I move close the child, who sleeps quietly again—and read the words embroidered on his shirt—BEVERLY HILLS DREAMING.

41.

"After you die, you wear what you are." —St. Teresa of Avila

Who are these people?

Squatters?

Are there others here that I don't see?

And is it possible that Hope lived here, too?

Or did the woman arrive after Hope's death?

I drift around the space again, keeping close to the floor.

There are plastic bottles of water and a few paper grocery sacks with packages of cereal and bread visible at the top. Some black plastic trash bags filled with something lumpy— maybe clothes.

A narrow door opens to a tiny room with a toilet and rust-stained sink.

Nothing I see makes me believe that the woman and her children have been or will be here long.

There's a stairway in the corner.

I rise through the ceiling to the second floor and find myself in another unlit space, the slightly open window blinds slicing the jaundiced radiance of the security light outside.

In one corner there's a queen-sized air mattress. Next to it a small table with an extinguished lamp on it and a folding chair.

Rose appears through the ceiling and joins me as I pause over the mattress.

A thin pillow without a pillowcase, a thin folded blanket and a folded sheet rest demurely at the foot.

No way to tell whose bed this is—or was. But the almost

geometric tidiness could indicate that Hope was here.

I float over to the table.

No personal belongings. No papers or books. No pens.

Just a Spanish-language newspaper creased crisply and perfectly in half.

Under "La Ciudad" a headline says, "Trabajadores de la Confección se Defienden." I am not sure what that means— except that workers are being defended. Food workers? Confectionary workers? Defended by whom?

A faint ringing sound reaches us from below.

I follow Rose as she sinks through the floor to the space downstairs.

A small flashlight burns in the corner, illuminating the woman, who sits up and fiddles with a small electric alarm clock.

Under the flashlight's LED beam, the woman's long straight hair gleams blue-black. Her eyes look dark. How old is she? Early twenties? Her impossibly smooth caramel-brown skin and soft round face make it hard to guess her age.

Rose drifts back to the mattress where the two children remain asleep.

I stay where I am—suspended a few feet below the ceiling.

The woman rummages in one of the paper sacks, takes out a red and white box of powdered milk and a plastic bottle and pads barefoot to the small bathroom.

She returns with a bottle full of milk and places it on the floor. More rummaging in the paper sacks produces a mug, loaf of white bread in polka dot plastic, a plastic knife, two paper plates and a jar of peanut butter. She pours some powdered milk into the mug—same deal—and returns with a cup of milk which she puts on the floor next to the bottle and the plates of food.

"Despierta queridos," she whispers as she crawls onto the mattress and kisses the baby's face and then the cheeks of the older child.

Why is she waking them now?

I move until I can see the clock—4:33 a.m.

Is she taking them somewhere? At this hour?

The woman changes the baby's diaper, takes the older one to the toilet, dresses them both in clothes she removes from a trash bag, and then disappears into the small bathroom.

She emerges after a few minutes with her face damp and her hair pulled back with a rubber band. She sits on the floor and puts on socks and tennis shoes, then grabs a sweatshirt from one of the garbage bags.

It is only now that she gives the children their food.

I'm surprised that the baby is old enough to hold his own bottle and to feed himself pieces of the bread and peanut butter.

The children eat in silence—their eyes big and reflecting the flashlight's glow.

Rose approvingly watches the children take their nourishment.

Then the woman prepares two more sandwiches, refills the mug and the bottle, and places them on the floor near the sleeping bag. Then she removes a bottle and a spoon from one of the bags.

The bottle looks like cold medicine—full of a dark green or maybe purple liquid. "Abrir bien la boca," she says and the child opens his mouth.

She measures two spoonfuls and feeds them to the child. Then she gives one spoonful to the baby, then puts the medicine and spoon away, picks up a hoodie from the floor and walks to the door.

"Sé bueno. Silencio. Te amo."

She bestows a backward glance at the children sitting in the corner of the room, then slips out the door and vanishes into the dark.

42.

"O death! We thank you for the light that you will shed upon our ignorance." —Jacques-Benigne Bossuet

At first I think that the woman ducked out for a cup of coffee. Not a good idea to leave the kids alone—but understandable.

But so little happens in the next twelve hours that I begin to feel that—except for the two small living children in this place—Rose and I are back in the world the dead.

Hour after hour the children doze quietly on the mattress with Rose just above their tousled heads.

Behind the blinds, night whitens slowly into day.

When the little clock says 6:49 a.m., I wonder if the woman is gone for good.

If she has abandoned the children here.

Or maybe killed them with whatever was really in that bottle.

I check to see if they are breathing—their chests rise and fall slowly—but the sleeping children are otherwise motionless.

What if the woman is already far away.

Shit.

If she wanted to dump her kids—then this is the place—shuttered, quiet and out of the way.

11:07 a.m.—Their breathing is faster. The children move around as they dream.

1:18 a.m.—The children are awake. They eat the food the woman left for them on the paper plates. They drink the milk.

3:46 p.m.—They sit on the sleeping bags but their eyes return to the door every few minutes.

6:22 p.m.—As the light fades, and the oldest child finally

crawls off the open sleeping bag toward the door.

The baby begins to cry.

The child crawls back to the sleeping bag, then hands the baby the empty bottle, which he begins to suck.

The baby's cry distresses Rose. She tucks her tail between her legs and her ears flatten. Then she gives me a wide-eyed sideways look that means, "Do something."

And I do what I have been doing hour after hour—

I stare at the children.

I watch the fucking clock.

I listen for the whine of sirens in the distance—for the sound of a key scraping the lock or for shouting outside the door.

I imagine the door being kicked in—hoping that Central Division has received an anonymous 911 call reporting two small children locked in a storeroom downtown.

But the hush remains unbroken.

The children cradle each other on the sleeping bag—holding hands—and facing the door.

Except for two unearthly presences—one canine and the other human—floating above them like auras—the children meet the returning darkness alone.

43.

"Either death is a state of nothingness and utter consciousness, or, as men say, there is a change and migration of the soul from this world to another. Now if death be of such a nature, I say that to die is to gain; for eternity is then only a single night." —Plato

At 8:20 p.m. the door opens and the woman enters.

Rose sails toward her, tail wagging in welcome.

The woman runs through Rose and almost drops the two white McDonald's bags she carries as hurries across the slippery floor toward the children.

She drops to her knees, places the bags on the sleeping bag, and switches on the small flashlight.

Then she kisses their cheeks, their ears, their hair—their hands and feet—murmuring in Spanish.

The children press their small faces against her neck. The older child jumps up and almost dances across the room and back for a hug.

The woman frantically changes the baby, refills the bottle with instant milk and water, then reaches into the MacDonald's bag and takes out a lidded cup with a straw in it—maybe a milkshake—and hands it to the older child.

She unwraps small burgers and packages of French fries, and tears the burgers into pieces.

The woman sits cross-legged on the floor and watches the children eat, then removes a burger from the bag and takes small, slow bites.

Perhaps it's the harsh light of the flashlight—but she looks exhausted. Her eyes seem sunken, her face puffy and drained of color.

When she is finished and the children have finished, she gathers the bags and food wrappers, picks up the flashlight, and walks toward the narrow staircase. "Quédate aquí," she says.

They remain on the sleeping bag while Rose keeps watch.

I follow the woman up the narrow stairs to the room with the table and the air mattress.

The woman peeks in as if she expects that someone will be there.

Then she sweeps the empty room with the flashlight's beam.

The woman frowns. Then she tiptoes down the stairs and joins the children.

"Agua," the boy says, holding up the mug.

The woman smiles and—tucking the flashlight under her arm—and carries the mug to the bathroom.

She comes out with the mug of water in one hand, the flashlight in the other. As she hands the cup to the little boy, the flashlight beam moves over the mug.

Wait.

The mug looks like a Judy Morganthal.

Years ago I saw mugs with a similar design in Grace's studio. I remember Grace telling me that her mother had made them for the family to use.

The mugs were never exhibited or sold.

On the round-handled cup, two little girls in stylized pinafores—one with red hair, the other with black hair—dance among brightly-colored flowers under a painterly glaze.

44.

"I think of death as some delightful journey that I shall take when all my tasks are done." —George Eliot

A Morganthal mug could mean that Hope was really here—and that by leaving it, she wanted to demonstrate to someone—to Grace?—her connection to this place.

Or the mug could have been placed here after Hope died.

By someone who knew Hope.

Or the people who broke into Grace's apartment.

The Gordo Locos.

But why remove something from Grace's condo and bring it here?

Grace told the police that nothing was missing from the condo—but was she sure? There was so much broken pottery on the floor—she could have made a mistake—and the news that Hope had been shot shook and confused her.

As I try to make sense of things—my eyes return to Rose.

She floats above the woman and the two children—her ears alert to their soft voices—her eyes full of kindly interest.

Finding Palo Pinto Street and this god-for-fucking-saken place and this sad woman and her poor drugged children has revealed three melancholy—maybe heartbreaking—things to me.

1. The woman and the children are here because they are in some kind of trouble.

2. The woman has some connection to Hope.

3. And whoever scared the life right out of Hope is still out there—and is a threat to Grace.

45.

"Death is a friend of ours; and he that is not ready to entertain him is not at home." —Francis Bacon

Rose and I have removed ourselves from the desolation and desperation of Palo Pinto Street—and returned—not to the comforting, silent, static blankness of the afterworld—but to the living turbulence that is Grace.

They still have a police officer stationed outside her condo. This time it's a female officer with a white-blond butch haircut, a thick, solid build and freckled cheekbones.

Rose and I travel through her faster than projectiles move through Jell-O—and then through the locked door—where we find what I've been yearning for—Grace.

She stands on bare feet and leans one shoulder against the door—unaware that her long-lost love and his companion-in-death have entered her residence uninvited and unannounced and shimmied right through her.

Grace wears a t-shirt and yoga pants in blackish, navy-bluish shades of mourning. Her hair looks damp—I remember how it smelled after a shampoo—like orange blossoms and almonds and pumpkin pie mixed together.

I see that her toenails—her fingernails are bare—are painted with battleship gray polish.

One of Grace's hands is on the doorknob—as if she is about to turn it and escape—the other holds a small white cardboard box.

I imagine that inside the box is one of her mother's vases salvaged from the break-in and packed lovingly in bubble wrap—maybe a mug like the one I just saw at Palo Pinto

Street.

"Absolutely not," Grace says quickly. "There will be no funeral." Grace frowns to emphasize the finality of her disapproval.

Officers Ventresca and Ang sit on the futon—spines straight, hands folded in their laps like middle school students caught cutting class.

Officer Ang's mouth forms itself into O as if she is going to say something—then changes her mind.

On the coffee table in front of them is a brown bag folded closed and secured with string. Two tags hang on the strings.

One is a bright orangey red with a black biohazard symbol printed on it—the other is the color of French vanilla ice cream.

Rose drifts past Grace and the police officers toward the bedroom—I presume she is searching for the tuxedo cat.

Now John comes out of the kitchen with a tray on which is perched a French press full of bright green tea and four cast iron Japanese teacups. "Anyone want stevia, lemon, raw sugar, or raw, organic buckwheat honey?" he asks as if this is his condo and the table upon which he places the tray belong to him.

It doesn't—nothing in this place is his.

"No thank you," Officer Ang says.

"Ditto," Officer Ventresca says.

John pushes down the plunger in the French press and returns to the kitchen.

I stay where I am—as close as possible to Grace where she stands near the door.

Officer Ventresca speaks. "We hit a dead end with the weapon, Miss Morgan. Your sister purchased the Glock at a gun store in Burbank. I was hoping the gun might lead us to someone who could tell us what might have driven your sister to do what she did."

Grace says nothing about this information.

Now it is Officer Ang's turn. "The gun is still at the Medical Examiner's property office. If you want it, it will have to be registered under your name."

"You don't want it," I say quickly. Maybe I'm shouting.

"I want the gun," Grace says.

Officer Ang looks surprised, "Okay."

"Why?" I ask Grace soundlessly. "Why the fuck would you want the gun? Are you going crazy? What do you even know about guns, Grace? Having a gun lying around is dangerous. The cops won't be here forever. What if whoever broke in returns? The Gordo Locos? And you're home? And they find the goddamn gun? Then what?"

Grace removes one hand from the doorknob and with both hands pulls the cardboard box close to her chest.

"And we checked the address on your sister's drivers' license," Officer Ang continues. "But it's an empty warehouse downtown on Palo Pinto Street—a place where squatters sometimes stay. The license was issued only three months ago. And we've found nothing connecting your sister to anyone at the NHPD station or to that address."

Squatters.

So maybe the woman and those kids have nothing to do with Hope.

"—She could have been depressed," Grace says. "Maybe she wanted privacy. I don't have any idea where she's been living the past few years."

Privacy?

Why force the cops to shoot her in the most public of all places—a police station?

"Do you remember the spray paint on your walls?" Ventresca asks.

I look around and notice that the red gang signs have been painted over with white paint—courtesy—I imagine—of the ever-so-handy and helpful hipster assistant John.

"Of course."

"The markings looked like some we found near the address listed on your sister's driver's license."

Grace's expression is opaque.

But she is quiet and still—which means that she is listening carefully.

"The marks could tie your sister to a gang—a dangerous gang downtown—also to what happened here in your condo," Ang says.

I can tell by the way her pupils darken slightly—and by the way she lifts her chin—that Grace is considering the implications.

Ang nods at Ventresca.

"It would be extremely useful to our investigation if we could see who shows up at your sister's funeral. Her toxicology report was negative for drugs, so this might be the only way we have to figure out how your sister could have become connected to this particular gang, how that gang might have contributed in some way to her death, and why the gang came here."

"The tea is ready," John announces. He tilts hot, jade liquid into each of the four cups.

The cups of tea immediately and obligingly release four columns of steam. John closes his eyes and sniffs the steam, "It's a Meizhan White and Fujan green mix. From San Francisco." John opens his eyes and looks directly at Officer Ang.

I get it now. Officer Ang is Chinese.

John won't stop, "I love the mix of oolong and the creamy finish. I think you will, too. It's a stress reliever."

Officer Ang takes a sip and offers a noncommittal, "Thanks."

Is this John person fucking kidding?

No.

He fucking isn't.

He apparently thinks it's normal and sane to behave like a fucking tea sommelier? Is he selling this shit?

How can Grace stand being around this schmuck?

The smug tea-maven John moves from sitting cross-legged to standing—without the use of his arms—goes into the kitchen, and returns quickly with a white plate on which is a pile of raw almonds, a pile dried apricots and some apple slices arranged in a half-circle. He places the plate near the teacups and then sits down on the floor again, the eyes above the hipster beard assuming a sly and meditative squint.

"My sister was cremated," Grace says.

She carries the box in both hands to the table where she places it next to the paper bag and opens the top flap.

Now I get it—the box does contain a Morganthal—Hope.

Inside the box is heavy gauge plastic bag of gray ash secured with a zip tie. The bag has a sticker on it and a tag is secured to the closure. There is a long sequence of numbers on the tag and the sticker, and same three numbers below proceeded by "CR".

"Inside that plastic bag is what's left of Hope," Grace says with a bitterness and anger I know too well, "or as the crematorium director called it, her 'cremains.'"

Grace begins to pace. "Did you know that even though the incinerator burns at eighteen hundred degrees, after hours and hours of burning there are still pieces of bone? Or that they filter out the bone—or dental fillings the woman said—and put the ashes in a fucking grinder?"

Ang, Ventresca and John stare sadly—each for his or her own reason—at the bag inside the box and do not answer Grace's question.

Grace stops pacing and crosses her arms across her chest. "Watching them put her into the oven—they called it a 'retort'—Did you know they open and close it with a remote control? Like a garage door? And then waiting for hours until the burning was over and then waiting for her to cool, and then to be filtered and ground, then tagged, bagged and boxed—was enough leave-taking for me."

Officer Ang clears her throat.

"Then what about a small memorial honoring her memory?" Ventresca says quietly.

Grace does not reply.

John lifts the plate and tilts it toward the officers. They shake their heads. Then he carefully counts out four almonds and two dried apricots, opens his mouth, and places them on his tongue.

As he does this I see that he that has a tongue piercing—no two—small silvery balls at the edge of his tongue's pink and pixilated tip.

Jesus.

It could be the piercings but John is one of those people who chews each mouthful maddeningly slowly and thoroughly.

And when John finally decides that the time has come to swallow an obliterated morsel—the tattooed writing on his neck wobbles up and down.

"You could pick a location that was important to your sister," Ventresca persists, involuntarily staring at John's neck as he embarks upon the slow-motion-mastication of an apple slice. "That would honor her and be meaningful to you, too—maybe it would help you find closure."

"There's no such thing." Grace doesn't shout, but her words are delivered with a fiercely scornful look at Officer Ang. "I learned that when my mother died. And my father. And then again when my—my friend—was murdered."

46.

"Death is not extinguishing the light; it is putting out the lamp because the dawn has come." —Rabindranath Tagore

Five living days ago Grace placed a notice in the *L.A. Times* 'Deaths' section stating the date of Hope's birth, the date of her death, and noting that a "brief and informal celebration of Hope Morgan's life" would be take place at the Blue Ribbon Garden at the Walt Disney Concert Hall at two o'clock this afternoon.

Grace and Officer Ventresca sit in the front of the plain wrap police car parked in the Walt Disney Concert Hall structure.

Officer Ang sits in the back.

She and Ventresca are in plain clothes. Ventresca wears a greenish-black polyester suit and dark blue tie. Ang wears a gray pantsuit and with a white blouse underneath and a string of pearls.

They look like cops.

And the car—with its siren light visible in the back window—looks like a cop car.

But maybe I think this because I know who and what they are. Perhaps they could pass for a cop couple on a day off here to enjoy a Sunday afternoon concert.

Grace sits in the passenger seat, the small health-food store bouquet of white roses in brown paper that John bought resting on her lap, and Rose has curled up above in the space above her head.

Grace wears what she always seems to wear these days— loose black pants, a black blouse and soft, flat black shoes.

"You're sure this will help you find out why Hope did what she did?" Grace says to Officer Ventresca. "Because that's the only reason I'm participating in this farce."

Grace is frankly unhappy and tense—coiling and uncoiling a curl of silvery-black hair with her long fingers as she speaks.

"We can't promise anything, Ms. Morgan." "But right now this is our only chance to shake something loose," Officer Ang says.

Grace frowns and she stares out the car window.

A jet-black Escalade with gold trim speeds into the aisle, then carefully straddles two parking spaces. The personalized license plate says, "GrnPlanet."

Officer Ang looks at her watch. "How many RSVP's?"

"I didn't ask for RSVP's," Grace says. "I have no idea who Hope's friends were."

Grace is prickly.

Of course, being prickly is her M.O.

But the memorial—whatever it involves—can't help but make obvious—to her and to everyone else—her long, deep estrangement from her sister.

Another car enters the parking aisle.

An impossibly shiny silvery Lexus that parks a few cars away from GrnPlanet.

A short, trim, balding man gets out of the car, then reaches in for his suit jacket.

"That's Alan Bardman." Grace says quietly. "The last time I saw him he had hair."

The officers, Grace, and I watch Alan Bardman, Esquire remove his jacket from the passenger seat and put it on—very nice pearly gray silk—then check his cell phone before stepping in his highly-shined dress shoes toward the escalators.

Rose doesn't seem interested in the lawyer—but she remains alert—having entered the quiescent, inward-looking state she so often assumes when we are alone together in the afterworld.

The three living human beings sit in the car for a little while

107

longer.

More cars arrive and disgorge passengers.

It's impossible to tell who is here for the concert, to look around, or to celebrate the short life of the mysterious Hope Morganthal.

"It's almost two," Officer Ang says.

"Let's roll," Officer Ventresca says. "Are you ready, Ms. Morgan?"

"I'm as ready as I can be," Grace says.

47.

"Birth was the death of him." —Samuel Beckett

Grace walks about six paces ahead of the officers out of the parking structure. Grim faced, she holds the bouquet with one hand like an umbrella—blooms pointing down.

Ang and Ventresca are a step behind her on the escalator, while Rose and I stay above her head.

Grace hurries off the escalator, and strides quickly across the lobby to the huge glass doors that open onto Grand Avenue. As two men enter, she slips outside, threading her way through people taking selfies with the building's luminous, curving panels as backdrop.

On the sidewalk Grace turns toward Second Street, then turns again and ascends three wide flights of concrete stairs.

Ventresca takes the steps two at a time and reaches Grace as she achieves the last step. Ang is with them in a moment.

At the top of the staircase—hidden from the street—I'm surprised to discover a garden that curves around the building.

I lived in L.A. all those years and never knew about this place.

A homeless man in a parka and torn jeans—or what I realize only appears to be a homeless man after his quick nod to Officer Ventresca—sits slumped on a bench under a flowering tree.

As Ang and Ventresca follow Grace around a paved path, they come upon a gardener raking a flowerbed.

Again an almost imperceptible acknowledgment tells me that this man is a cop, too.

After another turn, Grace reaches a small courtyard whose centerpiece is a rounded-edged, aquamarine mosaic fountain shaped like a lotus or maybe a full-blooming rose.

An inlaid series of letters proclaims that this is The Blue Ribbon Garden.

Grace was smart to pick this place.

It's small and contained—invisible from the street below, and from the other areas of the garden.

The police will be able to observe and track anyone who comes here to remember Hope—or anyone who just wanders through.

John the assistant—dressed in a long-sleeved white dress shirt, short black Argyll jacket and—get this—a fucking kilt and boots—stands next to the fountain holding a sheaf of photocopied sheets of paper with Hope's photo and some writing on them.

The kilt reveals John's pale, muscular and hairless calves, both heavily tattooed, the right with a navy-blue dream-catcher—the left with a red and black skull with flaming eye sockets.

I wonder what this schmuck has tattooed on his hairless buttocks. The masks of comedy and tragedy? Yin and yang? Coke and Pepsi?

A small table with a white cloth on it has been set up next to John. On it sits an open guest book, a pen and a vase—a Judy Morganthal painted with roly-poly nudes and oversized red and orange flowers.

Grace joins John at the fountain and hands him the flowers. He puts the papers on the table and unwraps the bouquet, quickly and efficiently arranging the white roses in the vase.

Now that we're close to the fountain I see that the small, irregular tiles are not a uniform blue at all. The flower's surface is covered by thousands broken pieces of that Dutch blue and white porcelain—what's it called?

My grandmother collected that stuff. A candy dish. A pot for plants with a blue windmill painted on it and a candy dish with flowers. Plates with Dutch scenes that she hung on the breakfast nook wall.

Delft.

"Good. You brought the guest book," Grace says to John. "Did Alan Bardman sign it? Make sure that people write down their addresses, okay?"

"Don't worry" John says. "Everything's cool," John says.

"Where's the chaplain?"

"Susan should be here any minute," John says. "She texted me a little while ago. There was an accident on the ten. But there's something I should tell you."

"What?"

"She's not a chaplain—yet."

Grace frowns.

"But she's starting chaplaincy classes this summer. Right now she's the sous-chef at the restaurant. You'll like her. She'll be perfect, I promise."

Grace is about to say something when a tiny old woman approaches her agonizingly slowly, steadying herself with a large, three-footed cane after each step.

"Gracie. Gracie Morganthal. Do you remember me?"

Grace stares at the gaunt woman, her dyed red hair pulled so tightly into a tiny bun that her white scalp shows.

Misery tightens the muscles in Grace's face, but she forces a smile. "Mrs. Beatty. It was very kind of you to come."

"Of course I came," the woman says. "I wouldn't miss saying goodbye to Hope. Before your parents split up, you and Hope practically lived at my house. I remember how cute the two of you were in your matching polka-dot two-piece bathing suits swimming in my pool."

Before Mrs. Beatty can share another memory, John touches Mrs. Beatty's tiny elbow and urges her toward the table. "Please sign the guest book, Mrs. Uh—"

"Beatty," the woman says, "Laura Beatty. I'm Gracie's neighbor from the old days."

"Cool," John says.

"And who are you?" Mrs. Beatty asks. "Grace's husband?"

What the fuck? The woman is obviously senile.

"I'm John," John says. "I'm Grace's studio assistant. I'm also a mixologist and a life coach."

Is there anything else Mr. Tongue-fucking-pierced-fucking-kilt-wearing tea-brewing life-coach doesn't do?

John holds the book so that Mrs. Beatty can sign it, then guides her to a white rented party chair, helps her sit, and hands her one of the photocopied papers.

As the sun appears from behind a ragged cloud, the fountain's mosaics flash an oceanic indigo.

Grace hugs herself.

Is it cold?

48.

"For life and death are one, even as the river and the sea are one." —Kahlil Gibran

The rented white chairs unfolded opposite the fountain are fully occupied now. Officer Ang sits in one near the back.

Officer Ventresca sits in the front next to Mrs. Beatty.

The undercover police officer dressed as a gardener repeatedly rakes the gravel in around a rose bush at the periphery of the courtyard.

The people seem ordinary. Unremarkable. Like a stock photograph come to life: —white, brown, African American and Asian—and a mix of ages.

Some are dressed for a funeral. Others are "business casual."

Are they Hope's friends?

A few approach Grace, murmur something, and then sit down.

And there is a small group who must be artists or friends of John—wearing black jeans and black t-shirts.

I don't see anyone who looks like a vandal or a gang banger.

Alan Bardman has placed himself a few feet away from the fountain under a flame tree—and looks deeply at the surface of his cell phone—not at the paper John gave him, which is visible folded in two in his breast pocket.

I rise above him and look into his phone to see what important worldly thing it is that demands his full attention.

Bardman is slicing fast-flying fruit with a virtual knife that he controls with swipes of his fat index finger.

Rose floats above Grace and John, who stand near the

fountain with a young, round woman in a long, batik skirt, and boots, who has a crocheted powder blue yarmulke secured with Bobbie pins to the long brown hair on her head.

"John told you that I don't want to speak, right?" Grace says as she pulls a folded paper from her pocket, and hands it to the woman. "Could you read this poem, then do a brief non-denominational, nothing too religious—service, and invite the others to say what they want about Hope?"

"Of course," the woman says, glancing at the paper. "John already filled me in." The woman has very pink cheeks, as if she's just been milking a herd of goats—and wide, white, straight teeth. She seems genuinely nice.

"I'm deeply sorry for your loss, Grace," the woman says.

"Thanks," Grace says quickly, and then, "I really appreciate you doing this."

Susan, sous-chef and chaplain-to-be, smiles and gives Grace a hug, which—I'm surprised to see—Grace accepts.

"I'm happy to help you out. John has told me—has told everyone at the restaurant—all about you. You're all he talks about."

49.

"Death is just a change in lifestyles." —Stephen Levine

"Hope Morgan's sister, Grace, has asked that I begin by reading a poem," Susan begins, and reads, "'I am not resigned to the shutting away of loving hearts in the hard ground. So it is, and so it will be, for so it has been, time out of mind: Into the darkness they go, the wise and the lovely. Crowned with lilies and with laurel they go; but I am not resigned."

I watch the faces of the mourners assembled here above ground. Their throbbing hearts—loving or indifferent—are hidden from view.

Alan Bardman stares into the back of the head of the man sitting in front of him, his cell phone forgotten for a moment in his hand.

"Lovers and thinkers, into the earth with you. Be one with the dull, the indiscriminate dust," Susan continues. "A fragment of what you felt, of what you knew, a formula, a phrase remains—but the best is lost."

"Down, down, down into the darkness of the grave gently they go, the beautiful, the tender, the kind; quietly they go, the intelligent, the witty, the brave," Susan reads. "I know. But I do not approve. And I am not resigned."

50.

"I still live. Pretty." —Daniel Webster's last words.

A mockingbird bird sips water from the rose fountain and squawks as Susan says "resigned."

Silence follows bird's voice and then the rustling of the papers with Hope's photograph on them.

The silence grows heavier as Grace stands, removes a single white rose from the vase, turns to the fountain and drops it into the still pool, returns to her seat next to John and folds her empty hands on her lap.

Rose floats above Grace's head as she does these things.

"Hi, everyone. I am Susan Rubino," the chaplain says. "I'm a chaplaincy student here in Los Angeles and I'll be facilitating this celebration of Hope Morgan's life."

John has put on shades and sits with his knees pushed primly together under the hem of his kilt.

Rose remains above Grace's head but her eyes are wide, scanning—for whom or what I do not know.

Grace adjusts her sunglasses and sighs heavily enough to make her shoulders droop.

"Hope Morgan was a daughter, a sister, a friend, and a colleague," Susan says. "I'm sure that each of you here knew her in a special way. So I'd like to begin this memorial gathering by inviting you to share your memories of her."

Immediately Mrs. Beatty struggles upright from her chair and, leaning on her unwieldy cane, slowly achieves the few steps to the fountain, turns and looks into the upturned faces of the group.

"My name is Laura Beatty. I lived next door to Hope and Grace's mother, Judy Morganthal, when she was Judy Roberts. Years and years ago. Before she was an artist. Or famous or anything like that. When her daughters were very young. I knew them well. Hope and Grace. They fit their names. They were both smart and darling girls. Good girls. Strong girls." Mrs. Beatty falters. "And I'm sure Hope had a good reason for doing what she did. Well, that's all I have to say."

John helps Mrs. Beatty back to her seat.

A very pretty African-American woman in her in a beige pants suit and pearls walks to the front and speaks next. "My name is Bernice Green. Hope and I were roommates in law school. Hope was just great. Brilliant. Organized. Type-A, if you know what I mean. And I'm the opposite. I'm totally disorganized. But we got along and became best friends. And I loved her. Hope could have practiced any kind of law she wanted, but she chose to help people who'd been evicted. We lost touch as the years passed—I joined a litigation firm—but I've always felt close to Hope. And I know I always will. Her discipline, integrity and generosity inspire me every single day." Tears cover Bernice Green's cheeks. "I just wish I could have done something."

The tributes continue.

From another college friend.

Another law school colleague.

A man from the Bayside Legal Aid Center in Santa Rosa where Hope worked years ago helping tenants.

Hope was beautiful.

Hope was brilliant.

Hope was good.

Hope was a very private person.

Intense.

With impossibly high standards.

Hope disappeared from my life.

I wish I had been there for her.

Hope stopped answering my emails.

I wish she had reached out to me.

I wish.

I wish.

The last any of these people saw or heard from Hope was years ago.

Nothing they say can possibly be useful to the police—or to me.

When they have finished speaking, Grace rises from her folding chair and steps quickly to the white table, takes off her sunglasses, glances coldly at Officer Ang, scans the group, and stares—without realizing it—at me.

"I want to thank you for being here. For supporting me during this difficult time. But most of all for being a friend to my sister, Hope. And I want to thank Susan, for the beautiful service."

Susan embraces Grace once again as Alan Bardman moves quickly in front of her, nods curtly at Grace, and starts to talk. "My name is Alan Bardman. Hope and I were engaged a long time ago, but it didn't work out. Hope fell in love with her job. She might as well have become a nun—that's how crazily committed to social justice Hope Morgan was."

Is it me or does Bardman sound more bitter than sad?

"Hope devoted her life to her clients. The chronically homeless. Undocumented workers. The mentally ill. The destitute. Drug addicts. Hope tried to do the impossible—to achieve justice for powerless people with intractable problems. It was only a matter of time before Hope had to realize that she couldn't win. That what she wanted to achieve was impossible. I imagine that she became despondent. That's why I'm not surprised, really, that things ended for Hope the way they did."

51.

"Death followed by eternity the worst of both worlds. It is a terrible thought." —Tom Stoppard

Bardman strides away from mourners who sit in bewildered silence as he disappears along the curving path that will return him to the stairs.

No one follows him.

Not even the cops appear interested in anything more he might have to say about the late Hope Morgan.

Susan assumes her place in front of the fountain. "This is really hard, isn't it?" she says. "To lose someone as wonderful as Hope Morgan is unbearable, but to lose her the way you've all lost her brings the deepest anguish."

Susan takes a breath as Rose passes shadowless over her head and toward the elevated garden's edge.

I follow Rose and look down at Grand Avenue three stories below.

"It's natural to be angry," Susan's voice counsels. "To blame the person we've lost for leaving us with so much grief and with so many questions."

Below us tourists take cell phone pictures of the concert hall and of themselves on the steps leading to the lobby.

A tour bus driver stands outside his bus and has a smoke.

A young woman pushes a fruit cart along the sidewalk.

"And we may never have answers. But we have to keep on loving Hope and we have to love and to forgive ourselves. I never met Hope Morgan but I'm sure that is what she'd want. I thank you all for being here today. May I ask you all to stand and join me in the Lord's Prayer—"

Rose floats over the rooftop's edge and into the air above Grand Avenue.

"Our Father, which art in heaven,

Hallowed be thy Name.

Thy Kingdom come.

Thy will be done in earth,

As it is in heaven."

I drift over the street with Rose and gaze as she does toward City Hall.

I see more tourists milling around.

A homeless man pulling a shopping cart piled full of plastic bottles, rags, tarps and aluminum cans jaywalks across Grand, stopping traffic.

'Give us this day our daily bread.

And forgive us our trespasses,

As we forgive those that trespass against us.

And lead us not into temptation,

But deliver us from evil.

For thine is the kingdom,

The power, and the glory,

For ever and ever.

Amen."

On the east side of Grand Avenue, a young man wearing a baseball cap and sunglasses sits in the driver's seat of a beat-up white Volvo station wagon and stares at the concert hall entrance.

Something about the Volvo is familiar but I can't figure out where I could have seen it before.

But one thing I'm sure of—next to the man in the driver's seat is the dwarf I saw on La Moda Street.

52.

"We are ignorant of the Beyond ...Just as ice cannot know fire except by melting and vanishing." —Jules Renard

The billowing, sail-like stainless steel panels of the Disney Hall seem to deflate under the origami-folded-down-the-middle utilitarian white roof hidden from the street below.

Rose and I remain high above Grand Avenue and wait for Officers Ang and Ventresca—or the undercover cops—to arrive at the bottom of the stairs and to notice the occupants of the white Volvo parked directly across the street.

I am eager for the police officers to become curious—or to recognize these men from a previous encounter.

The guy in the Volvo can only be here for one reason—Grace.

Who the fuck is he?

What does he want?

To stalk her?

To hurt her?

Why?

Rose barks sharply and I look back at the Concert Hall.

Grace, John, and the two police officers appear at the top of the stairs and begin their descent.

Grace has her head down.

John is talking to Officer Ang, who nods in his direction.

Officer Ventresca trots down the stairs, scanning the sidewalk as he does.

Officer Ventresca lifts his chin and gazes across the street where the Volvo is parked.

As he does, the driver quickly turns his face away from the

window and toward the dwarf in the passenger seat.

Now John, Grace and Officer Ang have reached street level. Ventresca bestows a backward glance at the Volvo before he turns and follows them inside the Concert Hall.

The Volvo driver turns his head to watch Grace and the others enter the Concert Hall lobby.

Grace could be going directly to the parking structure escalator inside or stopping for coffee at the snack bar.

Should I follow her?

Or shadow the dwarf and the Volvo driver?

I look at Rose—but she doesn't return my gaze.

Her iron-dark eyes are in the on the men in the white Volvo.

53.

"And here and there the unbodied spirit flies." —Ovid

Following the Volvo south through the downtown streets has brought us to an alley behind La Moda Street.

We pause as the man parks the Volvo under a battered No Parking Any Time sign near a scuffed-dirty yellow door, then follow as he and the dwarf walk down the alley and around the corner to La Moda Street

The gang signs the dwarf sprayed on the metal shutters along La Moda Street are hidden now that the shutters have been rolled up.

Living people crowd the street—talking, sipping cold drinks in paper cups, eating candy —moving shop to shop, open to the street and overflowing with handbags, shoes, scarves, quinceañera dresses in pale ice cream colors, jeans, pink, turquoise, yellow and white paper flowers, luggage and Halloween costumes—and shaded with brightly-colored awnings and rainbow umbrellas.

I've heard about this open-air marketplace, but I've never been here before now.

In life I avoided shopping. Especially for clothes.

When I absolutely needed something, I'd go to the Big Guy Shop on Cherokee off Hollywood Boulevard.

Bill Dale, the proprietor, was large.

Six foot seven and four hundred and fifty pounds. Big head. Big beard. Big hands. Big ass. Big, raspy laugh.

Bill was fat but fit. A former football player and Marine, he also owned a cavernous army surplus place off Melrose.

There's nothing here that would have been my style—or size.

And as we drift above the two baseball hats—one tall, one low—that protect the heads of the Volvo driver and the dwarf from the angled sunlight—I do not see even one item for sale that any of my ex-fucking wives would have deigned to touch with the tip of a smooth, manicured fingernail—much less haggle over or purchase with cash at a huge discount—which is the appeal of a place like this.

Only the absolute best for my ex-wives—only the exquisite.

Only shit bought with platinum credit cards slipped inside silk-lined zippered pouches inside purses made of endangered animals—ornate, high-end crap displayed inside air-filtered and perfumed Beverly fucking Hills boutiques with their bullet-proof electronically locked doors operated by uniformed security guards who ostentatiously carry loaded weapons on their narrow hips.

The dwarf and the tall man thread their way through the crowd of shoppers down La Moda Street until they stop at a tiny, narrow storefront loaded floor to ceiling with cheap suitcases, purses, backpacks, toys, belts, flip-flops, and beach balls—inflated and uninflated. More merchandise hangs from the ceiling—stuffed animals, collapsed baby strollers, skateboards and razor scooters.

A young woman with painted-on black upside-down V's for eyebrows and heavy black eye makeup sits on a stool in the back and taps the screen of her cell phone.

Next to her is a small cash register on a table and next to it a stack of narrow boxes covered with a pink terrycloth towel.

"Sylvia," the Volvo driver says. Like the dwarf, he wears a plain white t-shirt, baggy shorts, sneakers and white socks pulled up over his knees.

A low growl rumbles from Rose's gaunt belly when the man speaks, but she glides past him to the stack of boxes near the girl and hovers there.

The girl looks up nervously and shoves her cell phone into the pocket of her skin-tight jeans.

"Mateo." The girl directs the word at the Volvo driver—not at the dwarf who standing behind Mateo like a shadow.

Sylvia jumps off the stool and stands, waiting for Mateo to speak.

"Dónde está Andreas?" Mateo says.

"Andreas se fue hace un rato. Él dijo que iba a la fábrica."

Shit.

I have no goddamn idea what they are saying. What is a "rato"? Does "fabrica" mean fabric?

Mateo tilts his head toward Sylvia as if to indicate she's forgotten something.

Sylvia flushes pink from her forehead to her neck as she removes a chain with a small key from around her neck, and uses the key to unlock the cash register's drawer.

Mateo and the dwarf watch closely as Sylvia retrieves a thick, white envelope from the back of the drawer and then gives it to Mateo.

As she hands the envelope to Mateo I see that it is full of cash.

But Mateo doesn't bother to look. He shoves the envelope into a pocket in his shorts and turns toward the exit.

The dwarf nods at Sylvia, then turns to follow Mateo.

As he leaves the shop, Mateo removes various items from the wall displays and hands them to the dwarf—a huge white teddy bear, a pink umbrella, and a large curly-haired doll in a cardboard box.

I'm right above Mateo as he exits into the narrow, crowded street—until I realize that Rose floats over the towel-covered stack of boxes at the rear of the shop.

"Rosie, let's go."

Rose stays where she is.

I glide to the rear of the tiny store. "Come on Rosie," I urge.

Sylvia is talking into her cell phone now and the only word I understand is "Mateo."

Rose keeps her eyes on the pink towel that covers the boxes.

"We need to go. Now." I say, trying to sound reasonable, patient and persuasive. "For Grace."

The sound of Grace's name releases Rose's gaze from the boxes.

She directs a long serious look at me, takes a last glance at the pink towel, and follows.

54.

"The taste of death is upon my lips… I feel something, that is not of this earth." —Mozart

Rose and I drift a few inches above Mateo as he threads through the late-afternoon crush of shoppers on La Moda Street.

His arms balancing the items Mateo pulled from the shop's display, the dwarf struggles to make his way.

Mateo stops, waits for the dwarf to catch up, then pulls the huge teddy bear from the dwarf's embrace, and drops it in a nearby trash receptacle, repeating the operation until the dwarf is free of the umbrella and the doll.

At the end of La Moda Street, Mateo does not return to the alley where he parked the Volvo—he continues walking until he reaches Grand Ave.

Mateo and the dwarf do not speak or change their southerly course until they arrive near the empty L.A. Trade Tech College campus—and Palo Pinto Street.

55.

"Death is the dark backing that a mirror needs if we are to see anything." —Saul Bellow

The shadows are darkening, lengthening. Grand Avenue is almost empty of traffic although there are only a few cars parked on the street.

What day of the living week is it? Sunday? Saturday?

Downtown L.A. is—excuse the expression—dead on weekends except for gentrified places or tourist spots like La Moda Street, Chinatown, Little Tokyo and Olvera Street.

"Vamos a ver Andreas?" the dwarf says. I was beginning to think that the dwarf was mute. His voice is deep.

"No, tontopollas, vamos a Disneyland," Mateo says. I don't know what he's saying but the sarcasm in his voice makes me think that tontopollas means something like fuckface or shithead.

Then—to Rose's surprise—Mateo spits a pearly oyster of phlegm on the pavement.

The dwarf doesn't ask any more questions.

He follows Mateo as he turns a sharp corner and then turns again into an alley and waits with exaggerated impatience for the dwarf to catch up.

I notice a tall Dumpster has GLs spray-painted on it— Gordo Locos—just like the tags I saw on La Moda and Palo Pinto Streets and on the walls of Grace's apartment.

Instead of walking past the Dumpster, Mateo moves to one end of it, the dwarf on the other.

It must be empty. The two men easily slide it down the alley a few feet to reveal a closed metal shutter behind it marked

#11.

The sun drops behind the blank, two story buildings on either side of the darkening alley as Mateo raps quickly on the metal shutter.

In reply to Mateo's knock, someone rolls up the shutter from the inside.

It's a compact Asian man in khaki pants and a white button-down shirt who waves Mateo and the dwarf inside.

56.

"Afraid? Of whom am I afraid? Not death. For who is he?"
—Emily Dickinson

Rose and I melt through the wide metal shutter as it rattles its way back down to a cement floor.

Mateo and the dwarf follow the Asian man to a dark, narrow staircase at the back of the room.

I look around at the long, windowless space.

A flickering fluorescent fixture illuminates the cardboard boxes piled ceiling-high.

Machinery hums somewhere in the building.

The three living men do not speak as they climb the stairs.

Rose and I are silent too as we float straight up toward the low ceiling.

I'm quiet because I'm thinking.

Who or what connects Mateo and the dwarf to Hope—to Grace?

Who the fuck is Andreas?

Rose is not just quiet—she is somber—and her downcast eyes are solemn.

I promise myself to return to the shop and find out why those shoe boxes matter to her.

57.

"Birth in the physical is death in the spiritual. Death in the physical is the birth in the spiritual." —Edgar Cayce

Rose rises nose-first through the first-floor ceiling and I follow her into a cramped and noisy factory.

Women and men wearing paper surgical masks operate industrial sewing machines, heaps of unfinished fabric and finished pieces piled high on long, narrow work tables and the floor below.

I know about places like this.

My family's business, AndyCo., sells trademarked Happy Andy clothing and souvenirs—many of them manufactured in Mexico. And since my death and my shit brother's approval of a merger with MultiCorps—the crap they sell is probably being made by children in sweatshops in Sri Lanka or Thailand.

This sequestered factory might as well be one those—except that here the people working wear real shoes instead of flip flops, appear to be adults, and probably make more than twenty-five cents an hour.

Some or all of these workers are probably undocumented. That would explain why they keep this place hidden.

The dwarf, Mateo and the Asian man walk single file in the narrow aisle between the work tables toward the back of the room.

As they make their way, a plump, middle-aged woman with her hair pulled back in a ponytail rises from the stool behind her sewing machine, pulls her face mask off her nose and mouth, and stands. The Asian man shouts at her, "Sin

132uicer132132 ahora. Vuelve al trabajo!"

Rose flinches.

I know what "trabajo" means.

The woman quickly sits down, pulls her mask on, lifts some fabric from a huge pile of cut pieces and resumes working the machine.

I glide to her work-table and Rose accompanies me.

Above the mask, her smooth, caramel-colored forehead flushes with anger, frustration or embarrassment. The woman keeps her eyes on the fabric she guides under the quick jabs of the big machine's dancing needle.

She quickly completes final seam on a cream-colored t-shirt. When she finishes, she flips the shirt right side out and reveals the black block letters embroidered on the front—

BEVERLY HILLS DREAMING.

58.

"I do not fear death. I had been dead for billions and billions of years before I was born, and had not suffered the slightest inconvenience from it." —Mark Twain

The baby I saw at Hope's address on Palo Pinto Street wore a t-shirt like this one.

Is it possible the baby's mother works here?

The Asian man raps twice on a door at the rear of the factory floor, and opens the door.

I journey with Rose over the workers' bowed heads—scanning for the woman from Palo Pinto Street—as Mateo and the dwarf enter small, back room full of papers, cardboard boxes, dress forms, filing cabinets and a large desktop computer.

Rose positions herself near the ceiling above the BEVERLY HILLS DREAMING magazine ads and posters tacked to one of the walls. The young, female models in these ads are white, Asian, African American and brown—all gaunt-faced with flat chests that reveal the bones under their smooth skin. Girls in plunging v-necked sleeveless BEVERLY HILLS DREAMING t-shirts smirk haughtily at the camera lens—the cake-frosting coral Beverly Hills Hotel appearing to be leaning toward them in the background.

The same girls—their impossibly long waxed legs in short shorts and their feet in four-inch heels—shove their hands into the pockets of their BEVERLY HILLS DREAMING hoodie sweatshirts as they stare bitchily at the Beverly Hills sign. And in the poster behind the desk, four young male models wearing BEVERLY HILLS DREAMING wife-beaters soar above Rodeo Drive on airborne skateboards.

Behind the sleek glass-topped desk littered with fabric samples sits man who looks about the age I was when I died.

But that's all we have in common.

He's opaque. I'm see-through.

In life I was a schlub. And being shot and three years' dead hasn't done much to improve my looks.

Or my goddamn mood.

This man—is he Andreas?—is tan, tall, very handsome, lean, muscular—and ostentatiously alive. His long, straight spine and piercing brown eyes make him seem about to spring out of his seat and perform an athletic feat of some kind—maybe do a quick one hundred one-armed push-ups or a fast three-mile sprint—and then slide back into his office chair—without perspiring or a taking a deep breath.

He holds a cell phone to his ear and writes something down on a legal pad.

"Uh huh," handsome says, nods at Mateo and the dwarf, then writes some more. "And the polyester denim summer blend?"

The man wears a tight, white t-shirt under a linen jacket. The letters ERLY HILLS DR are visible between the stylishly crumpled lapels. He has the sleeves of his linen jacket rolled up to reveal tan, hairy, beefy forearms.

I know what's bothering me—this guy is just like my shit brother.

The rolled-up sleeves—I hate that—the forearms with just the right amount of arm hair so that he looks manly instead of primitive.

Good-looking men like these are always the ones who front operations like this.

Smart, hungry, men with an instinct for business.

Maître d's.

Politicians.

Businessmen.

Realtors.

All of them entrepreneurial.

Tough-minded.

Ambitious.

Confident.

Predatory.

Assholes.

Okay. Maybe I'm bitter because in life I was a failure.

Not handsome.

Not successful.

Not driven.

With the wrong amount of hair on my arms.

And on my ass.

And with nothing to show for having lived.

I mean it.

I squandered my life.

The effect of my time on earth was exactly—nil.

Thirty-goddamn-eight long years dissipated in a few seconds—poof—just like a fart.

59.

"Death is a problem that can be solved." —Peter Thiel

Mateo shuts the door and sits in the straight wooden chair opposite the desk. Instead of taking his hat off, he turns the brim around to the back.

The dwarf remains standing behind him, his hat brim pointing forward, his eyes on the floor.

"The shipment absolutely cannot arrive in Mexico past the deadline. Do you understand? And I expect to see the culottes by seven a.m. tomorrow," Handsome demands, "the denim blend and the rayon." He disconnects his cell phone and looks at Mateo. "The sister?"

"La hermana, she went with the nine-one-ones to the coroner. Then another day all the fuckin' way to fuckin' Van Nuys. The gabacho and some cops sat in the car for like three hours while she was inside there—Comfort Cremation Services. Then she comes out with a little cardboard box. Since then, the chica does nothing, Andreas. Nothing."

Okay—Handsome is Andreas after all.

Progress.

"Nada," Mateo continues, "and even at the servica funerario, she's always with nine-one-ones or her Maricón

Hermana means sister—Hope's sister—Grace.

The nine-one-ones must be the police.

Maricón? Who the fuck knows what that means? Maybe he's talking about John.

Rose has positioned herself behind me.

I suppose she doesn't realize that Mateo, Andreas and the

dwarf cannot see her. Cannot hurt her.

The large muscles under Andreas's angular jaw contract, then release a few times before he speaks. "I don't give a shit what she does. Just what she knows. You're sure the sister didn't tell her anything?"

"We never saw nothing—"

Andreas interrupts, "—No? Can you swear that bitch never talked to her sister?"

Mateo shakes his head.

"Then kill her. I want her dead before the next shipment."

60.

"If you don't know where you are currently standing, you're dead." —Samuel Beckett

Rose and I have fled your fucked-up world for the merciless peace of our little hideaway deep within the uncharted territory of the dead.

Here—where there is nothing except Rose to touch—my fingers feel.

"You're a good girl, Rosie," I say. "You're the best."

Rose wags her tail and rolls over onto her back in the airless space front of me—her paws relaxed, her feathery tail swaying leisurely like an aquarium fish's delicate dorsal fin.

Rose observes me dreamily as I run my cracked, gray fingers through the thin fur on her bony chest and think about what I know—

Hope found out something about Andreas that was very dangerous to know.

The Gordo Locos—or at least Mateo and the dwarf—know what it is.

Mateo and the dwarf have some interest in that La Moda Street schlock store—does Andreas, too?

He must—Mateo asked Sylvia where Andrea was.

Andreas runs Beverly Hills Dreaming.

And maybe that shop on La Moda Street.

Mateo and the dwarf, Sylvia, Hope, the woman and the children hiding out on Palo Pinto Street—Andreas is connected to all of them.

How?

Rose turns over again and stretches her legs.

Hope dedicated her life to lost causes—isn't that what people said?

Did Hope represent a factory worker in a contentious legal case against Beverly Hills Dreaming?

And what do the Gordo Locos do for Andreas, anyway?

The gang controls—and maybe extorts the businesses in the neighborhood—Didn't I see Mateo collecting that envelope from Sylvia?

Maybe they keep Andreas's workers in line.

And what kind of shipment was Andreas talking about?

If it's only clothing—why would Hope or the Gordo Locos give a fuck?

Drugs.

And I know shit about drugs.

Food was my drug.

In life weed depressed me.

Alcohol didn't agree with me or I with it—

With me it's have one drink. Flush. Become enraged. Pass out.

Unlike my shit brother who could handle anything and did—I avoided psychedelics, drug dealers, and pills.

So I have no real idea what a shipment of illegal drugs might be or where it might be going.

Cocaine? Heroin? Ecstasy? Pills?

Rose looks at me quizzically—one ear higher than the other—as if she's a dog stretched out in front of a cozy hearth instead of here where she is stretched out in front of what is basically eternity's abyss.

As I scratch the soft places behind her ears and then the top of her head—my fingers discover a matted tangle of fur that requires scissors to remove—but I don't have those here.

"Poor, Rose," I hear myself say, "Hope saw something. Or heard something. Or someone told her something. Probably about Andreas's drug shipment."

I've decided drugs are it.

"And Andreas found out."

Rose's tail registers my words with a series of approving,

metronomic swings.

"Or Hope discovered something on her own—maybe about a gangbanger or a worker who was involved in smuggling—or about Andreas himself. Whatever she learned was lethal for her to know. And rather than waiting around to be killed—and endangering Grace—she found a way to end her life."

But I cannot speak the next words aloud.

I can only think them—

Hope was wrong about protecting Grace.

And now—because Andreas thinks she knows what Hope knew—they need Grace dead.

61.

"In the night of death, hope sees a star, and listening love can hear the rustle of wing." —Robert G. Ingersoll

I need to be with Grace.

Always Grace.

Especially Grace.

But Rose and I hover above Mateo and the dwarf instead.

Their baseball caps are still turned backwards as they sit inside Paul's Kitchen, an old Chinese restaurant that occupies part of the first floor of the Bow An Association's two-story ancient pigeon shit-speckled off-white building on San Pedro Street—walking distance from Beverly Hills Dreaming.

The place is set up like a diner—a long counter with stools and some booths—and the walls are a faded salmon. Pepto Bismol pink "oriental" panels screen the windows. Dodgers memorabilia, photos of Tommy Lasorda and lucky cats are arranged on shelves behind the counter. And there's a dusty lucky horseshoe nailed above the door.

Mateo flicks Tapatio sauce onto a mound of beige chow mein flecked with grayish meat, then jabs it with his chopsticks. "You never saw the bitches together, did you?"

Instead of answering Mateo's question, the dwarf scrapes the brown sauce floating around a pale island of egg foo yung onto his spoon, and then licks the gelatinous liquid until it's clean.

Rose shows no interest the food below her on the Formica table.

When I was alive I read somewhere that dogs are nose-driven—their world is a world of scents assaulting the thousands—or is it millions?—of special olfactory receptors inside their nasal passages.

But sweet, dead Rose can't smell a goddamn thing.

And I suspect that her indifference to food comes more from having been slowly starved to death during her time on earth than from being a ghost.

The dwarf shakes his head, no.

"The one in WeHo. Did anyone ever see her around the neighborhood?" Mateo taps his chopstick on his water glass.

The slim Chinese waiter who looks about eighty shuffles slowly to the table.

"Mas, por favor," Mateo says, indicating an empty bowl on the table next to a tiny dish containing a mixture ketchup and pale ochre Chinese mustard.

The waiter returns with a bowl of crispy noodle sticks.

"Thanks," Mateo says, mixing the ketchup and mustard together with a noodle before popping it into his mouth.

"Did you?" Mateo asks again.

"Nel," the dwarf says.

His voice is surprisingly, incongruously, and weirdly deep. Jesus. He sounds like an announcer on the Spanish radio station.

The dwarf licks more brown sauce off his spoon, and then attacks the anemic-looking egg foo yung. "But the hermana, esé, she could have sent a letter to her sister. Or an email, no?"

Mateo's expression darkens. "Que? You told me you didn't find nothing in the condo."

"llevanate," the dwarf's voice rumbles from somewhere inside his barrel chest. "Just saying the bitch could have. We one-eight-seven her—and maybe el Maricón La mañana."

62.

"Despise not death, but welcome it." —Marcus Aurelius

It's tomorrow in your mutable world.

Or as the dwarf might boom—la mañana.

I don't know what one-eight-seven means—but I can guess.

Today's the day they plan to murder Grace.

As if my attendance in the living world could protect her—from them or from herself—I have left the afterworld with Rose to keep watch.

To stay close.

And you won't fucking believe where we are.

Where Grace Morgan has chosen to spend this dangerously bright morning in October.

Not in Santa Monica with a gallery director.

Not at a cold press 143uicer or fucking tea place or an organic coffee roaster or inside her studio planning her next reality-altering, mortality-obsessed, performance piece.

Not at Petco buying hairball medicine or more litter for the cat.

Not teaching her seminar at USC.

Nope.

She's in the Hollywood fucking Hills.

At Mount Sinai Cemetery to be exact—standing over one of the thousands of flat grave markers that interrupt the broad, ascending grounds.

Yellowish crab grass has spiderwebbed the edges of the flat marker Grace has chosen to visit.

No exhausted flowers droop over the edge of one of the

green plastic vases the funeral directors make available in a stack by the cleverly disguised-as-a-tree-trunk refuse container with a little water spigot in front.

No pebbles or stones indicate that mourners have visited this grave—recently—or ever.

Grace stares down at the marker as if she can see through it to the earth's crust and layers—and then all the way down to the molten core.

Or as if she's looking deep into a well in which she's dropped something irreplaceable—maybe her great-great-grandmother's diamond and emerald and ruby and sapphire engagement ring.

I look beyond Grace and locate Rose's delicate silhouette against the hill above us—she skims a section of freshly mowed and watered grass—her feet churning above the sparkling blades.

A police officer in plain clothes stands about forty feet away from Grace near the small wooden sign alerting visitors to watch for coyotes, snakes and bobcats. His sunscreen-slathered shaved head glistens in the white autumn light that glances like broken glass off his wraparound shades.

Another officer—a trim, brunette woman—sits in a parked plain wrap police car, the front wheels turned toward the curb on this steep road.

If there are other police officers around, I don't see them.

Workmen in blue uniforms excavate a fresh grave below us. Their truck is parked at the bottom of the hill—near the elaborate, wrought iron entrance gate.

If it could my shriveled heart would be thump against my shattered ribcage.

Grace shouldn't be out in the open like this.

That's what the officers told her on the way here.

But Grace insisted.

It was do it like this—her way—with the officers "giving her personal space"—or she would goddamn well come here alone.

They couldn't stop her.

And now here she is—her head bent over the grave marker—a confusion of dark curls obscuring her face.

"Forgive me," Grace says. "Please. Forgive me."

The yip of a coyote in the distance and the soft shush of cars from the road below us are the only answer Grace receives.

"I've fucked up every relationship that really mattered," Grace tells the silent bronze rectangle planted in the ground. "I pushed you away. You and Hope."

Grace puts her hand in the large pocket of her shapeless, loose gray linen jacket and removes a small, decorative pumpkin—the kind supermarkets sell near Halloween and Thanksgiving.

'Look around, Grace," I say. "Jews don't do Halloween."

Grace holds the little squash in both hands as if it were made of crystal.

I hear another yip and look toward the top of the green hill at the cemetery's perimeter.

A coyote stands in a tree's deep purple shadow at the top of the hill—Rose hovers above the tilted head of the lean, canine figure.

"I am so, so sorry," Grace announces to the empty air. "And I should have been here for your funeral. I just couldn't face it. Or your fucking family. But I realize now how wrong that was."

"Forget it, Gracie," I say. "Please. The funeral? I hated it. And the rest? Everything was my fault. Not just yours. You know what a putz I can be. Now go home. Please. I'm begging you. Go."

Grace stays.

She places the pumpkin on the grass, then brushes the crabgrass and dirt off the grave marker with her bare hands.

A black compact car travels sedately up the empty cemetery road, slowing slightly as it passes the parked police car.

A man in sunglasses, a dark sport coat and Panama hat drives the car. The curly blond hair of a girl is all that's visible next to him in the passenger seat.

The car passes Grace and continues up the hill toward a

fork, the smaller road leading to the largest and newest section of the cemetery, a steep area without trees and with big spaces between graves. The man stops the car to consult one of those maps they give you when you enter the cemetery—but which they call a "memorial park."

The man gets out of the car, removes two large supermarket bouquets from the car's trunk, slams it shut, and takes the flowers with him as he gets back into the driver's seat.

"Rest in peace," Grace says, then ceremoniously places the little pumpkin on the marker right above the first row of raised bronze letters on the marker—

CHARLES STONE

1974-2012

Always In Our Hearts

"I wish you knew how much I loved you," Grace says, hoarse.

"I do," I insist as my voice breaks. "I did. I love you, Gracie. Always and completely. Now please. Get the fuck out of here."

"I love you, Charlie," Grace says, then covers her eyes with her hands and weeps.

The man in the Panama hat suddenly turns the car around and speeds down the hill toward Grace.

63.

"A death-bed's a detector of the heart." —Edward Young

The car rushes toward Grace, then slows as the girl with the curly blond hair—and wearing a Halloween mask—aims a short black firearm out the open car window.

"Grace!" I warn soundlessly.

Grace doesn't look up until the bald police officer runs toward her, his firearm raised, and shouts.

"Halt! Drop your weapon!"

The girl in the mask squeezes the trigger as the driver accelerates down the hill toward Forest Lawn Drive and the freeways beyond.

64.

"Ending, where all things end, in death at last." —William Morris

The bullet locates Grace and knocks her off her feet.

She rests unmoving on her back—eyes shut—legs folded grotesquely—her sandals thrown off—her feet bare—and the little pumpkin knocked sideways to the grass near her.

There's a hole in the fabric of Grace's gray jacket—right where it covers her left breast.

The female officer speaks into a handheld radio. "Code three. Shots fired. We need backup and an ambulance."

Gun drawn and crouching behind the open door of the vehicle, she scans the area and then runs to Grace. She kneels—one hand holding her gun, other hand touching Grace's neck—as the bald officer pursues the shooter's car on foot, cutting across the rows of graves as he sprints toward the entrance.

65.

"I burned the candle at both ends and it often gave a lovely light." —Christopher Hitchens

Rose floats with me over Grace's body—she returned to me the moment the gun's report echoed through the cemetery.

The only woman I really love is dead.

By "love" I don't mean care for—I mean love in a flesh-burning, heartbreaking psychosexual way.

Now I wait—

For Grace to ascend—like perfume levitating over a cone of smoldering incense—from her static, crumpled doppelganger on the grass—straight into the afterlife—and into my lifeless, outstretched arms.

I don't know if I mentioned this before—but only the dead can see the dead.

Only the dead can hear the dead.

And only in the afterlife can the dead touch the dead.

What will Grace think when she first sees us?

Sees me?

What will she say?

As she slowly begins her journey into the afterworld—what will she do?

I am desperate to receive and to return her embrace.

To once again feel her body against mine.

But ours will be the merging of two shadows of shadows—the dance of two separate flames.

Grace won't know it—but we won't have much time.

Just a moment.

What we do and say then will be the last things we ever say

or do together.

Am I shaking?

I stretch my arms in front of me and look at my grayish hands.

Jesus.

My hands tremble as fresh gunfire crackles from behind the kiosk at the cemetery entrance.

Rose cocks her ears at the sound, then lifts her chin and opens her mouth to howl along with the shrill and swelling squeal of sirens approaching from Forest Lawn Drive.

66.

"I cannot say, and I will not say
That he is dead. He is just away." —James Whitcomb Riley

Black and whites block both the entrance lane and the exit lane at the wrought iron cemetery gate.

Uniformed police officers rush the entrance kiosk.

But Rose and I retain our airborne locations above my grave.

Above Grace.

The Shakespearean-tragic death-altering short-suffering long-ached-for-in-our-dead-hearts-and-loins reunion during which we profess our bottomless, abiding and mysterious post-mortal love—our ghostly fingers gratefully entwining—our pupils widening—our fading bodies mingling one with the other into one pale shadow—our mouths—our lips—our souls—if we have them—hungering—before Grace disappears forever and alone into eternity—never happened.

Grace—groaning and pissed off at the EMTs—is alive.

A female emergency technician opens Grace's loose gray jacket and undoes—with harsh ripping sound that disturbs Rose—the wide black Velcro straps that secured the thick black bulletproof vest Grace was wearing underneath.

I can see the place where the bullet ripped and cratered the vest.

"From one to ten, how much pain are you in?" the EMT asks, removing the heavy vest.

"Fifteen," Grace says, gasping for breath. "Twenty. Like I've been hit in the chest with a baseball bat."

67.

"…death rescues you from life." —Bangambiki
Habyarimana

Rose and I hover among the branches of a tall eucalyptus tree
near the entrance to the compost facility in Griffith Park.

A seriously large chained padlock secures the white metal
gate.

The cemetery shooter's black compact car is parked off the
road and behind the stand of trees below us.

Beyond the gate is an area with picnic tables, domed black
plastic composters and piles of leaves and debris in various
stages of decomposition set up for demonstrations. Three
shiny goldenrod yellow Department of Sanitation trucks sit in
small lot in front of a fenced area housing tall piles of dead
leaves and branches.

I assume the lifeless leaves and branches are what they use
to make the compost—but all I know about decomposition is
what I've learned from personal experience—which is to say
that I understand degradation in the literal sense and dispersal
and disappearance is our destiny. But so far all I know of the
process is subtle and escalating deadness.

As for the leaves—in case you haven't guessed by now—in
life I wasn't a gardener.

I don't think I owned a pair of sandals. Or shorts.

Ordering takeout Chinese and listening to Ramblin' Jack
Elliott or Kinky Friedman and the Texas Jewboys on my
stereo inside my little dark apartment in Hollywood would
have been a pretty full day for me.

Or driving to the Andy Co. offices and back to one of the

big houses I lived in with this or that ex-fucking wife or my shitty Hollywood apartment.

Rose reacts to the sounds of police sirens wafted from Forest Lawn Drive—the whisper of traffic of the 134 and the 5 Freeways—and thrum of a helicopter approaching from the east.

Mateo stands next to the car.

The dwarf gets out of the passenger side.

He pulls off the wig and then removes the mask from his face, which is pink from the heat. The dwarf shoves them into a black trash bag and picks up the Panama hat, sunglasses and dark sport coat puddled at Mateo's feet and pushes them into the bag, too.

Mateo taps a sequence of numbers into his cell phone. Despite the sirens, the helicopter's rumble, and the soft hiss of traffic—it is quiet enough to hear the tiny electronic ring inside his phone and the disapproving screeches of a scrub jay hopping in the brown leaves near the car.

Rose sinks a few feet above the ground to watch the dusty blue bird pull a worm from the soft earth and then hide it under some decaying eucalyptus leaves.

The ringing stops.

"It's me," Mateo says.

The plastic trash bag in one hand, the dwarf climbs through an opening in the gate, and trots up the road one to of the piles of compost, shoves the bag inside one of them, and then pats the compost back into shape.

"She's down," Mateo says as the dwarf returns. "That's all I know. We couldn't wait around to see."

The dwarf opens the trunk of the black compact and removes two dark blue baseball caps. He puts one on his head and tosses the other to Mateo.

Mateo catches the cap as he listens to the voice inside his phone and then says, "Later."

"Andreas es un culero," Mateo says, spitting on the ground for emphasis, then puts on his cap as the two men begin to jog away from the narrow road and up and over the dry hillside and toward hiking trails and Los Feliz Boulevard to the to the southeast.

68.

"All is forgotten in the stone halls of the dead." —Stephen King

Grace is down all right—still flat on her ass near my final resting place—if you can call being wedged into a wooden box and buried six feet below the grass "resting."

I don't.

Police, EMTs, a gaunt man wearing a badge that says, "Memorial Counselor" the three grave-diggers, a dead man and a deceased dog observe a blood-colored donut-shaped bruise around a dark indentation swell and turn purple below the nipple in Grace's left breast—under what must have been the place where the bullet met the body armor.

"They say that blunt force trauma feels just like that," the EMT says. "A baseball bat."

"They?" Jesus.

One of the EMTs starts an IV and injects what I assume is pain medication into the line, while another technician covers Grace's exposed chest with a sheet.

Grace groans groggily as they slide an orange backboard under her and then lift the board onto a gurney and into the waiting ambulance.

Rose begins to move toward the ambulance, but I shake my head and stay where I am—a few inches above the worried memorial counselor's thinning backcombed auburn hair—his mouth open like a fish—his hands folded unconsciously across his chest.

Rose looks at me questioningly.

Grace doesn't need me hanging around—

Doesn't need a mute, bloated, immaterial three-plus-years dead ex-lover and an undernourished ghost dog haunting her life.

The grave diggers—in no hurry to get back to work—lean philosophically on their worn shovels as the doors to the ambulance are slammed shut.

Rose looks at the ambulance and then looks at me.

Grace doesn't need me in the ambulance.

And you know what?

She didn't need me when the Gordo Locos tried to assassinate her.

Not now.

Not last year.

Not during all the years that she's lived in your world without me—or the years I've spent in the afterlife without her.

If Grace had needed me when I was alive—we would have been together.

And that's not what happened.

She had what she called "relationships."

I had a series of fucked-up marriages.

Ex-fucking-wives.

Ex-stepchildren.

And now I've become a goddamn voyeur.

Not even that.

A voyeuristic shade.

John the assistant will be with Grace soon—I'm sure of it— his body warm and real under his goddamn kilt—his arteries surging with oxygenated blood under his fucking tattoos.

He'll see to it that Grace has everything she requires.

Life coaching.

Green tea.

Brown tea.

Organic coffee.

Lentils.

Sympathy.

Sex.

There—I said it.

I—who have been permanently silenced—who doesn't fucking exist—a goddamned cadaver with a cadaver dog as companion—have acknowledged the thing I've been fighting not think about when I think about Grace—

Well fuck.

69.

"Death. It's around more than people realize." —Jessica Sorensen

The checkerboard pasture of Yeatsian April green Bermuda grass shivers in what must be a stiff wind below Rose's paws.

Her tail straight—her chin lifted—her mouth open slightly to taste the air she will never taste—her reddish fur unmoving—she glides over home plate and then sails up and over the bleachers—across the vast, empty parking lot—over the THINK BLUE sign—and returns for another exuberant pass over the empty field.

Death has emancipated Rose.

It is good to watch her and to not be at the cemetery—

Where Grace suffered.

Where my own grave and those of my grandparents and parents and many of their friends and acquaintances are neatly arranged along the irrigated, expertly mowed, snake-ridden, bobcat and coyote-infested hillsides.

The hazy city floats beyond Chavez Ravine like a Hiroshige cloud—the buildings just misty silhouettes in the fading afternoon.

City Hall.

The Cathedral of Our Lady of the Angels.

The high rise shaped like a giant nose hair trimmer.

The Department of Water and Power.

The Music Center.

The Disney Concert Hall.

And—although I can't actually see it from here—I know it's there inside the cloudy panorama—the narrow alley that leads to Beverly Hills Dreaming.

70.

"Our dead are never dead to us until we have forgotten them…" —George Eliot

Will I gradually diminish and deaden until I withdraw completely into obscurity?

Or will I persist unbidden a little longer—like memory—here in your world with Rose?

She floats unweary beside to me—chin lifted—her eyes mysterious and vigilant—and focused on the horizon—or something beyond.

When and if I achieve complete deadness—or merge with eternity—I don't want loose ends troubling me.

I want to revel in the massive, mind-blowing stillness with Rose—finally—in goddamned nonstop, un-illuminated insensate fucking tranquility.

Which I cannot achieve until I accomplish certain things—Grace's permanent safety is one of them.

And until I figure out others.

For instance—

Why Andreas was so worried about that shipment.

What Beverly Hills Dreaming is really doing.

It can't be just skinny jeans or hoodies or t-shirts.

It has to be something worth the Gordo Locos' time and interest—

Something worth trying to kill Grace for—

And worth literally scaring Hope to death.

Drugs.

It has to be.

Rose lifts her head and blinks.

But they wouldn't be smuggling drugs to Mexico, would they?

Even a drug-virgin like me knows that much.

No.

It's got to be drug money.

Shitloads of it.

71.

"The days carry the living along; the dead are left behind…"
—Juliet Waldron

Rose and I navigate the narrow space above the glass-littered and glittering pockmarked surface of the alley.

Four unadorned white trucks with orange and blue Baja California plates idle in early morning darkness that smudges the outlines of the unmarked Beverly Hills Dreaming factory entrance.

A male driver and a male passenger sit in the front of each truck.

They do not speak.

Some of the men wear baseball caps in dark colors. A few wear straw hats—the sort field laborers wear to shield them from the sun.

But there is no sun.

Rose flinches when the rasping corrugated metal door is rolled up from the inside.

Is it the high-pitched scrape of metal on metal or something else that bothers her?

The first-floor is stacked to the low ceiling with hundreds of identical tape-sealed white cardboard Beverly Hills Dreaming packing boxes.

The Asian man we saw before finishes rolling up the metal shutter and says, "Vámonos."

The men become active—hopping out of the trucks and stepping quickly into the warehouse.

The Asian man nods the men toward the back, where each lifts two or three boxes, carries them outside and loads them into the trucks.

As they work, the Asian man keeps his eyes on the trucks.

Rose's ears flatten and her body tenses. She releases a slow, rumbling growl as she darts over the men's heads and over the stacks of boxes through the crowded first-floor space toward the back staircase that leads to the second-floor factory and to Andreas's office.

I want to see the entire shipment loaded—and hear what the man says to the drivers—but I have learned to pay attention to Rose.

72.

"Any relic of the dead is precious…" —Emily Brontë

As I follow Rose into the second-floor factory, the sound of industrial sewing machines rumbles like thunder.

I'm a little surprised at what I see—a full crew of night shift workers—piece workers, sewers and cutters—mouths and noses covered with bandanas—heads bent over machines—piles of fabric and clothing at their feet.

Two men—a different Asian man and one with coffee-colored skin—stride back between the work tables.

"Más rápido!"

"Hazlo más."

What did I expect?

A goddamn drug lab?

Rose floats over the workers—avoiding the men as she makes a zigzagged circuit of the large room.

Then she repeats her movements, pausing finally over a sewing machine at a table in the back.

Rose lifts her head and looks at me wide-eyed and serious.

The men below must be almost finished loading the trucks and getting ready to go.

"Rose," I say, "Let's go back down. I need to see where those men are going."

Rose stays where she is, her eyes wide and fixed upon an empty metal folding chair in front of the work table as if she knows that in a second or two it will transform into the burning bush.

"Rosie," I urge. "Please."

Rose keeps her eyes on the chair as I begin my descent to the lower floor—

Until her sudden, insistent barks stop me.

I return in time to see Rose—her nostrils wide, her mouth open—hovering between the dark man and a young woman with gleaming, straight blue-black hair—the woman's back is to me—who stands near what was the empty work-table.

"Dónde has estado?" the man demands.

"Fui al baño. No me siento bien," the woman says softly.

"Nunca vuelvas a hacer eso," the man shouts, then—his hand passing through Rose—delivers a fast, hard, flat-handed blow to the side of the woman's face.

She stumbles, but rights herself, then covers her face with her hands.

"Vuelve al trabajo," he orders. "And don't stop working unless I say so."

Rose shows her teeth and growls as the man steps from the woman.

As the woman finally lifts her head and raises her dark eyes—her smooth, caramel-colored cheek a dark red from the blow—I understand what Rose wanted me to know—

This is the young mother from Palo Pinto Street.

73.

"Being dead is better than being dull…" —Ray Bradbury

The woman from Palo Pinto Street is upstairs sewing pair after pair of denim pant legs.

How much is Beverly Hills Dreaming paying her?

Eight cents a piece? A quarter?

Rose and I watch the men load the last boxes into the trucks and secure the roll-down doors—

I wonder where the woman's children are right now—

Are they still alone on Palo Pinto Street—or has she found someone to watch them?

Thinking about her kids makes me feel hopeless.

Hope-less is right.

Did she know Hope?

The men get into the trucks, but instead of driving off, they sit and wait.

After a few minutes, the bluish glow of low headlights clarify the alley, then the grumble of a matte-black Porsche stops in front of the unshuttered door.

The Porsche's door opens and Andreas unfolds his slim self from the car's glowing interior.

"Okay," Andreas says to no one in particular. "Nothing has changed. Nada ha cambiado."

A few of the men sitting in the driver's seats in the trucks nod their assent.

Andreas reaches into his car and takes a sheaf of printed papers from the seat. He gives the papers to the driver in the first truck. "El declaración de exportación del expedidor."

The driver accepts the papers and puts them into his jacket pocket.

"Mateo expects you at the customs broker in Otay Mesa in three hours. Tres horas."

74.

"…you'll be perfect when you're dead." —Dan Harmon

The four trucks make excellent time as they travel south toward San Diego—first on the 5 and then on the 805.

They stop only once—at a rest area near Oceanside to use the restrooms, smoke or stare thoughtfully for a few minutes at the cement-colored surface of the sea.

Rose and I linger above the last truck in the line and stay with it as it passes the defunct San Onofre nuclear plant—the twin domes glowing like pale breasts with erect nipples—as the sun climbs over the empty scrub and low mountains of Camp Pendleton to the east and silvers the flat Pacific.

The drivers are cautious—going a little above the speed limit—not more.

As they travel from the 805, to the 905East/Otay Mesa Exit, I realize that I won't discover what's really being transported in those cartons—or hidden somewhere inside the trucks—until see the customs inspection at the border or even later—until after the delivery in Mexico.

When the trucks arrive at the Callejón de Exportación/Frontera Internacional, I'm not completely at a loss.

My shit brother supervised the nuts-and-bolts AndyCo. Operations like exports, shipping and customs declarations—but I knew more than he thought I did—much more—though of course AndyCo. Shipped chazerai from manufacturers in Mexico to the U.S.—not like this—other way around.

The trucks arrive at the customs broker—I know enough

from AndyCo. That Andreas would have set up an advance clearance and invoice of the cargo long before the shipment left L.A.

And as Andreas said he would be—Mateo—sans dwarf—waits outside the large, low, modern building.

Mateo waves the trucks around the back.

After parking, the driver in truck one gets out and gives Mateo the paperwork. Mateo scans the papers, then turns these over to the broker—a short, overweight man in khaki pants and an Eduardo International green logo t-shirt who has emerged from one of the roofed parking docks.

At the broker's request, the driver opens the first truck and lifts out six of the cardboard boxes.

The customs broker checks the boxes' dimensions with a metal tape measure, and carries one to an outdoor scale and weighs it.

Finished with his inspection and calculations, the broker hands Mateo more papers—these must contain something I recall hearing my shit brother call a pedimento—an official classification of the cargo, including weight and dimensions for each unit.

The driver returns to his vehicle and waits while Mateo enters the building with the customs broker—where—from what I know—the shipments will be cleared and duties electronically paid.

After a few minutes Mateo comes out and waves the trucks on.

If I thought I'd see or learn something important here—I was wrong.

Rose and I resume escorting the trucks as they move on.

We travel south with them to La Media Road, then left as they their places in the horseshoe-shaped queue at the U.S. Customs' export facility.

The trucks advance at a creep until a male customs inspector wearing a black CPB vest and holster waves them through the U.S. Export booths.

Rose and I are still right with them as they rumble across the border into Mexico.

75.

"I am ready to meet my maker, but whether my maker is prepared for the great ordeal of meeting me is another matter." —Winston Churchill

As the trucks travel the mile or so to the Mexican inspections booths—I realize that I may be in luck after all—the cargo may be inspected one more time.

The trucks stop under the narrow, low-roofed structure.

The driver in the first truck hands the inspector the paperwork Mateo gave him at the customs brokerage.

The inspector waves a handheld computer over the documents—U.S. Shipper export declarations and registration forms—glances at the trucks, and then stamps the documents.

It looks clear.

Then the traffic signal ahead with dark green and red bulbs suddenly glows red.

The inspector scans the license plate of the first truck with the reader and then points to the secondary inspection area.

76.

"But what matter whether I was born or not, have lived or not, am dead or merely dying. I shall go on doing as I have always done, not knowing what it is I do, nor who I am, nor where I am, nor if I am." —Samuel Beckett

The driver's expression darkens. But he nods and guides his truck toward the inspection area, the other trucks following sedately.

This is my chance.

I sail ahead, eager to observe this final inspection up close.

That is I move—until Rose—her the hair on her neck bristling—opens her mouth, bares her teeth and snarls.

Waiting for the truck and its driver is a tall, extremely thin uniformed customs inspector—a patch with the Mexican flag on his sleeve—and a large, muscular German shepherd with deep black eyes that strains against a thick, black leather lead.

Is it the inspector or the dog that disturbs Rose?

The short, taut lead?

I drift closer to the man and the dog.

Rose hesitates—her eyebrow whiskers erect, her narrow body tense.

She watches the officer trot alongside the excited dog as it makes a quick circuit around the truck's exterior.

Then Rose floats to me—still wary—as the inspector leads the dog back to the driver's side of the truck.

"Abrir el camion," he says.

The driver exchanges a quick look with the man in the passenger seat, then hops out and opens the back of the truck.

The inspector leads the dog to the back of the truck, unhooks the lead, and says, "Encuéntralo."

The dog's nostrils widen and his tail begins to swing as he

greedily tastes the air spilling from the truck's interior.

Rose is fascinated now.

She gets what the dog is doing—or some of it.

Rose sails to the back of the truck and follows the dog as he rests his large black paws on the interior floor and then leaps into the narrow space between the cardboard boxes stacked to the roof.

The dog moves from box to box—intent—nose grazing the surface of each box before moving to the next.

Rose stays close and begins to mimic the dog's movements—she knows he's searching for something—she likes the game.

If I'm right and there's cash hidden somewhere in these boxes or in these trucks, maybe this drug dog will find it.

Drug money might carry scent of the coke or weed or whatever the Gordo Locos and Andreas are selling.

At the rear of the truck the dog tries to climb up a stack of boxes—sniffs—and then drops down and returns to the door, jumps down to his handler, and sits calmly—face on paws—on the cement floor.

Rose has followed the dog out of the truck and watches—her head cocked—as the handler attaches the lead to the dog again, pats the dog's angular head, and then directs the dog to the tires, the wheel wells and the truck's bumpers.

The shepherd noses each location on the truck—but fails to alert his handler at this truck or on the other three.

The inspection over, Rose aims a quizzical look at me.

"There's nothing hidden in there," I say. "Not a fucking thing."

77.

"The soul takes nothing with her to the next world but her education and her culture." —Plato

After Otay Mesa, Mesa de Otay, and a Tijuana shopping mall not far from the Mexican customs inspection station and that looks like it could be in Van Nuys—I watch Andreas's men park the trucks and unload the boxes.

Then Rose and I travel with Andreas' very important shipment to its final—no longer mysterious—destination— the back room of a Mexican department store where I see— finally—what is packed inside the Beverly Hills Dreaming cardboard boxes—culottes, t-shirts, hoodies and skinny jeans.

That is fucking it.

Oh and Rose watches a black-throated, white-chested, crested bird, with a long tail and hooked beak peck at an almost ossified chicken bone in the parking lot behind the loading dock.

Well after all that—it's time for us to hasten back to you-know-goddamn-where.

That's right.

The hereafter.

Where it's no birds, no chicken, no trucks, no cardboard boxes, no labor, no peace, no drugs, no drug money, no drug sniffing dogs, no fashion, no factories, no murder, no shoppers, no lovers, no cats, no tea, no cremains—

It's just Rose and me—the dirt nappers, the ones whose ghosts have been given up, the supposedly justly-rewarded, the farm-buyers, the flat-liners, the members of the invisible choir. The succumbed, the late, the stiffs, the living-

challenged, the dust biters, the whacked and the croaked—
and up to our eyebrows in nada.

Rose floats—her head on her paws facing away from me
and into the endless, colorless not-mist, not-fog, not-cloud—
into the endless nothing—her tail folded against her gaunt
form.

Since our return—I've been a bit preoccupied.

And Rose has been vague.

Distant.

As if she is weighing an important decision.

Or trying to locate the answer to a very difficult question.

To be honest, her turning away from me like this—for just
a little while—is a relief.

Sometimes the fierce forthrightness of her appraising gaze
is almost too hard to bear.

Like right now.

Which is why I look away from her and down at my bare
dead feet.

Or dead bare feet.

Why the fuck did I think I—so often totally wrong in life—
would get things right in death?

There was no drug money in that shipment.

Not a goddamn cent.

Not a peso.

The whole drug-cash smuggling operation I thought I'd
discovered?

Zip.

All that happened was that Andreas shipped boxes of
Beverly Hills Dreaming clothing to a retailer—a guy at Moda
Para Moda—who seemed very eager to receive the delivery—

So eager that he had the boxes unpacked and began stocking
his shop right away.

And I was wrong about that too—culottes are making a
comeback.

78.

"…there comes a point at which we must relinquish the dead, let them go, keep them dead." —Joan Didion

Though I've been wrong about almost everything, Grace is still in danger.

I need to figure out what was there that I didn't see.

Or what I saw and didn't understand.

"Where to start?" I say aloud as if hearing a human voice— even if it's only my dead one—will fortify my resolve and clarify my thinking.

Rose uncoils herself, stretches slowly, turns, then floats slowly toward me until her nose almost touches mine.

"I have no fucking idea where we should start." I say to Rose's heartbreaking and baffling eyes. "The boyfriend, Alan Bardman? Palo Pinto Street?"

Rose's ears flatten. Her whiskered cheeks puff with impatience.

"Hope? Grace? Beverly Hills Dreaming? The Gordo Locos? Drugs?"

The pupils in Rose's dark brown eyes enlarge and then darken to black.

"Or something I haven't figured out yet, right?"

But my question just hangs there in the absolute emptiness of the afterworld.

Rose is gone.

79.

"It was one of those rare times when remembering the dead was more important than tending to the needs of the living."
—Dean Koontz

Rose does not hover watchfully over the tuxedo cat dream-chasing rodents among the tangled sheets on Grace's unmade bed.

Rose does not haunt the hallway where a male uniformed police officer sits on a folding chair outside the door listening to the rain and sipping something hot from a paper cup.

Rose does not hover close to Grace who sits cross-legged on the floor—the standing lamp's yellow glow making the silver in Grace's dark hair look gold.

Grace is barefoot and wearing loose gray sweatpants and a loose sweatshirt.

Is she in pain from the injury to her chest? She must be.

Is she afraid?

I can't tell.

Hope's gun and the brown paper bag from the coroner's office are on the floor in front of her.

Grace takes a breath and then unties the strings, removes the tags—red and beige—and dumps the bag's contents on the floor.

80.

"The dead would not rise up because he took five minutes to drink a coffee." —James Craig

I look at the clothes Hope wore when she died—tennis shoes, jeans, t-shirt, socks, white underpants, two parts of the beige bra the EMT's cut in half and the baseball hat—tumble out of the coroner's bag slowly like a lumpy, coagulated liquid.

Grace gently touches the top of the jumble with both hands open flat, then she closes her eyes.

It seems like a long time passes before Grace opens her eyes again.

Has Rose left me for good this time?

Where is she?

With Mateo and the dwarf?

At Palo Pinto Street?

Or somewhere else entirely?

A place I will never know?

Grace lifts half of the bra off the pile and places it near her right foot. Then she takes the next thing—the pair of jeans—unfolds them, examines the murky blood stains across the thighs—and arranges them below the half-bra.

What does Grace want with the gun?

Why hasn't she put it away in a safe place?

Grace removes the tennis shoes, the socks, the other half of the bra and the underpants and arranges them on the floor—shoes and socks, then the jeans—until she's assembled a flat, bodiless version of a shirtless Hope.

Now she unfolds the crumpled, once-white t-shirt.

The front is now one red-brown stain interrupted by bullet

holes—the stain's edges bleeding pink.

Grace groans as she presses the shirt smooth with her hands in the yellow light and places it above the jeans, and then puts the gun where an invisible hand at the end of an arm sticking out of the shirt would be.

I drift close to Grace—

There is something dark under the dark bloodstains on the shirt—letters or parts of words—

BE E LY H LS DR AM NG

81.

"'Tis falsely said
That there was ever intercourse
Between the living and the dead." —William Wordsworth

Mumbled male voices in the hall, then the door opens and John enters the condo.

He flips a light switch and cool white light fills the room.

Raindrops glisten on John's beard and hair. His boots are water-darkened. "I brought dinner," he says, and lifts a take-out bag into the air to demonstrate. "Mung bean casserole from Hugo's. Your favorite."

Fucking really?

Since when has mung bean anything been even tolerable to Grace?

Now it's her favorite?

Grace raises her eyes from the morbid Flat Stanley arrangement of Hope's clothing and firearm on the floor. "I'm not hungry. I'm thinking. I'm working."

John puts the take-out bag on the table and kneels close to Grace—very close. So close that she must feel his breath on her neck.

So close that his shoulder touches her shoulder.

His thigh presses against her thigh.

John surveys the bloody clothing on the floor.

The gun.

"And all this?" John asks.

"This?" Grace says, her eyes sad and bright. "This means something. Something important. You want to know what?"

John nods to indicate not that he knows—but that he wants to know.

"This means that for the first time in my life, I know exactly what I need to do. Just not how to do it. Yet."

82.

"…let us deprive death of its strangeness…" —Michel de Montaigne

Jesus.

How fucking stupid and self-centered can I be?

Hope wore a Beverly Hills Dreaming shirt on the day she died.

And now I know what Rose wanted me to notice at the morgue—not me, my own mortality and my feckless love for Grace—but those brown bags holding the belongings of the deceased—

Now what?

Do I hang around while Grace shares her mung bean casserole with John?

But if I search for Rose—what guarantee is there that I will ever find her?

This isn't the first time Rose has abandoned me.

What if this time she doesn't want to be found?

I've already failed the test I didn't know she was giving me.

I've already proven unworthy of Rose's friendship.

Am I insensitive?

Fuck yes.

Selfish?

Yes. That, too.

What if Rose has lost patience with me?

Has she finally lost interest?

I don't even answer that question.

I know my thinking is magical—but all along I've felt that if I just stay close to her—Grace won't fall in love with John.

But if I ever want to find Rose and discover the reason for Hope's death—even if leaving means that the little love Grace still has for me is lost forever—

I must leave Grace now.

83.

"…always look on the bright side of death…" —Eric Idle

I know what you're thinking.

I know what you want to ask me.

Well, here's your answer—

Fuck no.

I haven't found Rose.

Or—maybe and more precisely—she hasn't permitted me to find her.

Yet.

I'm not with Grace, either.

I vamoosed out of the condo right after John began helping Grace out of her clothes.

Yeah.

My dead heart is as cold as the mung bean fucking casserole in a Styrofoam container that John stuck in the goddamn freezer.

But I'm clear on a couple of things—

I must find Rose.

Whatever it requires—I must find Rose.

And—to protect Grace—I must discover why Hope died.

Oh, and after all this time I learned something else about being dead.

Death is failure.

Death is loss.

Everything—who you are, what you know—goes.

Whoever you thought you were, you weren't and you're not.

And just for the fucking record—

When I choose Rose—a dead dog—my dead dog—and relinquish Grace, the one huge, true love I've had to her living lover, to her goddamned life—

I do not stop—I never stop—loving her.

84.

"We all have the same body, the same human flesh, and therefore we will all die." —The Dalai Lama

Jesus.

Being dead is so goddamned humiliating.

So mortifying.

At least mine is.

Maybe your death will be a goddamn breeze.

A fucking party.

And I can't stop thinking about Rose.

Her composure.

Her dignity.

She accepts her death—as she accepted her life of anguished solitude—with composure.

Although I know she isn't around, I can't stop my eyes from searching for her silent, nimble shape floating nearby.

Where the fuck is she?

Has she moved on to another dead soul—or is she finally on her own?

"Rose," I call. "Rosie!"

Nothing.

Just a smear of purplish stars behind dissolving clouds.

The murmur of rush-hour traffic disturbing the quiet on this narrow canyon road.

Just headlights glitterizing the wet, dark, leaf-scattered pavement.

I need to know what the Gordo Locos's deal is with Andreas and Beverly Hills Dreaming.

How Hope got mixed up with them and what Andreas is

hiding.

Oh, I still think drugs—not fashion—is Beverly Hills Dreaming's real business.

So I—who knew nothing about purchasing or using illegal drugs in life—find myself in the awkward position of having to find out now that I'm a ghost.

Which explains why I'm about to visit the living people I'd hoped my murder would allow me to avoid for all eternity and an infinity of eternities beyond—my shit brother Mark and his wife Helen.

The last time I saw him was when he'd figured out a way to make money off my murder and was holding a press conference courtesy of the LAPD Homicide division.

Something about a fund for troubled youth or overeaters or homicidal bicyclists that our family business AndyCo. Was establishing in my so-called memory.

It was just a public relations' scheme to help my shit brother and MultiCorps promote AndyCo. And foist its array of useless Happy Andy products on witless consumers.

What a dismal joke.

You'd think that being shot to death by a road raging bicyclist would be indignity enough.

Fuck no.

Here I am outside my unbearable shit brother's house once again—and just like old times—I'm trying to work up the courage to go in.

The house is a huge, expensive, exclusive, tasteful killer-view hillside number in the Beverly Fucking Hills end of Benedict Canyon.

I watch my shit brother guide a silver Tesla—with its custom HAPYANDY plates—up the short driveway, through his dead brother—to the faux rustic electrified gate.

After a moment the gate silently and majestically opens and my shit brother drives the Tesla onto his imposing and very private property.

The gate closes with an impressive thud.

I try to psych myself for what comes next—proximity to my

shit brother and his wife Helen—AKA the Loathesome Duo.

I stare at the Japanese maples. Their combustible orange foliage in the fading light—the raindrops sliding like amber from each star-shaped leaf.

I hear the Tesla's door shut with a soft, very expensive clunk.

Resigned, I pass through the gate, float over the little bridge—there's a rain-fed stream below it—and up the driveway, over the flagstone entrance and through my shit brother's massive, carved front door.

Well here goes fucking nothing.

85.

"What is there in thee, Man, that can be known?
Dark fluxion, all unfixable by thought…" —Samuel Taylor Coleridge

Helen—self-styled "interior designer"—has redone the place since my murder.

The mid-century modern showplace is now an Asian-themed, folk arty retreat with complete with Tibetan prayer flags and a sprawling open floor plan.

As I follow my shit brother, I can see across the huge interior to an infinity pool, outdoor kitchen, and a terraced hillside beyond.

Rose would love that hillside—wild and alive with scrub, oaks, hummingbirds, jays, hawks, coyotes and deer.

Still tall, still thin, still fit, still handsome and still smug—my shit brother steps out of his soft leather shoes—and walks—favoring the balls of his wide, highly arched sock-less feet—into his massive kitchen—all slate, stainless steel, marble, Japanese ceramics and folk-art masks.

"Helen?"

As I float above my shit brother's head, I notice a faint, thin, pink hairless scar interrupting his short haircut—indicating that he's overcome the Stone family male baldness syndrome with a recent surgical intervention.

Involuntarily, I touch the bald spot on my own dead head that's been there since my twenties.

Still there.

"Helen?" my shit brother calls again while he opens the Sub Zero and takes out one of the twenty or so glistening bottles of champagne inside—a long-stemmed, wide-hipped bottle of

Laurent-Perrier La Cuvee Grand Siecle.

"What?" Helen appears at the bottom of the stairs. She's barefoot and wearing a narrow black leather skirt and a turquoise silk blouse. "I'm exhausted. So this better be worth dragging me out of bed and away from *Entertainment Tonight*."

"Oh. It is. It. Is," my shit brother Mark says and grins. "Do you want champagne now or after you know why we're celebrating how fucking clever Mark Stone is?"

Something is terribly wrong with people who refer to themselves in the third person—they're assholes.

"Never," Helen says and sits on one of the high rustic stools arranged under the huge, salmon-veined marble island. "I feel faint. I haven't eaten anything since an apple and some unsweetened goat milk yogurt at six a.m. Really. Two sips of anything alcoholic and I. Will. Pass. Out."

So now we know that Helen wins the Who-Ate-The-Least-Food-Today Contest.

Aren't you glad that's been cleared up?

Helen's skin is soft looking ("Dewy"?) and surgically firmed over her enhanced cheekbones. Her injection-plumped cheeks are powdery pink, her hair freshly dyed and blown, her eye makeup applied to bestow a permanently shocked expression, and her pouty lips—wide and glossed—seem hungry for a chemically-engineered yet organic low-calorie health food that hasn't been invented just yet.

Mark removes a flash drive from his pocket and inserts it into a laptop sitting on the marble counter. "I'm not faint. That new pop-up Nordic fusion food truck came by the building today—the chef worked at Noma for god's sake. I had the wild herb and currant amuse bouche—he said he foraged the herbs this morning in Los Osos—the sea urchin and hazelnuts and—what was totally unbefuckinglievable—the berries soaked in vinegar for a year. A fucking year. Amazing."

Helen displays the anorexic's refusal to be impressed by ecstatic descriptions of food. She crosses her arms and presses her puffy lips together as the laptop screen brightens and a video begins to play.

A young red-haired mother stands at the stove stirring something in a small pot while an adorable redheaded toddler boy sits in a high chair watching her. After a moment she spoons the pot's contents—bright chemical yellow macaroni and cheese—into a cute blue plastic bowl and begins to sing the theme song to my late father's children's TV show:

> *"Happy Andy, Happy Andy, Oh what fun for you and me!*
> *Happy Andy, he's so dandy, Oh he never wears a frown!"*

The little boy smiles, begins to clap, and begins to sing along:

> *"Happy Andy, He's so funny, when he tumbles to the ground!"*

Just then who appears in the onscreen kitchen—courtesy of computer manipulation—but my dead fucking father—Happy Andy himself in his rodeo clown costume—singing the song's final line:

> *"Happy Andy is our Very, Very Favorite Rodeo Clown!"*

My shit brother pauses the commercial—freezing my poor dead father grotesquely open-mouthed at "clown"—and announces, "AndyCo.'s very first necro-ad. What do you think? The Multi Corps people were shitting themselves they were so excited about it. They project our instant and microwave pasta sales to increase by forty percent."

Jesus.

To see my father once again inhabiting the role he despised so much in life—and which brought him so much unhappiness—and to see him removed from the solitude of death and forced back into world of the living to sell instant macaroni and cheese—is monstrous.

"It's brilliant," Helen says, her goldfish lips parting slightly to signify approval. "You are a fucking genius."

"I am," my shit brother Mark says and refills his crystal flute with more champagne. "Here's to Mark Stone."

86.

"Every man must do two things alone; he must do his own believing and his own dying." —Martin Luther

A wall has been knocked out or some square footage added to create my shit brother's new (since my death) three hundred square foot master bath.

A huge black rectangular soaking tub occupies the middle of the marble-floored room.

Incredibly monotonous sitar music leaks from speakers embedded somewhere in the faux-finished walls.

The golden flames of little candles sparkle inside glass cups arranged around the wide rim of the massive tub. They direct their light on the shiny wet collar bones and the anemic, flat breasts of the naked woman in the tub—Helen—and on the hairless, thin, muscular, too tanned chest of the naked man— my shit brother Mark—who stands near.

I close my eyes.

I don't want to see Helen or my shit brother Mark ever— but especially don't want to see them like this.

I open my eyes—and immediately regret it.

Helen dries her bony, manicured hand on an embroidered towel, then lifts a large joint from a dish and ignites it with one of the little candles, and then places the joint between her mega-lips and inhales.

"Is it any good?" Mark asks. "Joshua said it was freaking unbelievable."

Who the fuck talks like this?

The man is almost fifty fucking years old for God's sake.

Helen removes the huge joint from her mouth and exhales

slowly.

"It's okay. Not great. That stuff last week was better."

"What stuff?"

"That stuff last week. Wednesday, wasn't it? Didn't you say Joshua said it was from Thailand?"

"Oh, that. This is supposed to be even better. Forty-five percent THC. Hundred and fifty dollars a goddamned gram. Let me have some." Helen passes the joint to my shit brother.

Mark closes his eyes and inhales.

I count to ten before he releases the smoke through his blue-white teeth, "You're right. This is crap."

"I know I'm right," Helen says and closes her eyes—the pupils dilating. "I'm always right."

"Are you ready?" my shit brother asks.

"Not yet," Helen says. "I don't feel relaxed yet. That whole thing I went through in Culver City today with the tile contractor about the fire pit and the outdoor pizza oven was a fucking nightmare."

My shit brother takes another hit. "I'm telling Joshua tomorrow that this is shit. Absolute. Shit." My shit brother puts the joint into the little china dish and climbs into the tub and lowers himself until only the top of his no-longer-bald head is above the steaming water.

"What about the coke?"

Mark doesn't hear her. Helen waits until his head appears above the steaming water and asks about the coke again.

"Good idea." Mark climbs out of the soaking tub again and walks—on the balls of his wet feet—his dripping wet erect penis leading the way like a baton—across the stone floor and to a distressed wooden cabinet, opens a drawer, and removes a small, intricately carved what-must-be ivory box.

His watery ball-of-his-foot prints reflect the candlelight as he carries the box back to the tub and gets into the water once again.

Mark opens the box.

Inside is a glass vial filled with white powder, a carved mirror and an ivory or bone spoon and straw.

"This should do the trick." Mark arranges two parallel lines of the powder on the mirror, and carefully offers it to Helen.

"Are you sure it's kosher to do tantric on coke?"

"Sure I'm sure. I read in *Rolling Stone* that Richard Branson did coke and tantric sex. On a fucking plane. We'll have to try that on our way to Bangkok."

Bangkok? They're going to Bangkok?

Helen arranges her balloon lips into a smile and then inhales a line into one perfectly round rhinoplasticized nostril.

"That's awesome," Helen says. "Very awesome. Hmmm," she sighs. "Very, very awesome. Can you get me some more?"

Awesome? Awesome doesn't mean "nice"—it means inspiring terror or dread. Awesomeness makes one feel small—insignificant in the face of something huge and mysterious and obliteratingly unknowable —it doesn't mean giddy.

And how can something—anything—be "very" or "very, very" awesome?

Jesus.

"I'll talk to Joshua tomorrow," Mark says again, snorts the last line, and closes the little ivory box. "Now, take a slow, deep cleansing breath."

Helen inhales and her very awesome bony chest expands and then slowly deflates.

"Okay, breathe with my breathing." My shit brother inhales and then exhales ostentatiously.

"Stare into my eyes," my shit brother tells his wife, his eyes widening as if in terror. "Don't blink."

Helen mimics his gaze and stares into the little greedy poisonous chasms that are my shit brother's eyes.

"Good," my shit brother says. "Now you're ready for a mind-blowing, totally spiritual tantric fuck courtesy of the very awesome AndyCo. President—and genius—Mark Stone."

87.

"It is not the strength of the body, but the strength of the spirit." —J.R.R. Tolkien

Don't ask.

Just don't.

Well if you must—I didn't hang around.

I slithered out of the living world—

And back here to place where I'm the star of my own goddamn necro-ad.

Here in the stern and sober, airless, brotherless, sexless—afterlife.

But I learned two things from my awesomely unpleasant visit—one big and one small.

The small thing's name is Joshua.

The big thing?

Rose is still gone.

88.

"I feel monotony and death to be almost the same." —
Charlotte Bronte

My shit brother expertly parallel parks his silver Tesla near a
sound studio on Lankershim Boulevard, then strides past a
yuppie wine restaurant—Decanter—and around the corner to
a small coffee shop without a name or sign next to a thrift
shop on Magnolia.

There's a line of people texting or staring into their phones
while waiting to get in.

Young women in leggings, scarves and puffy jackets. Men
that look like John.

I wonder what Grace is doing as Mark takes his place at the
end of the queue, stands on the balls of his feet and checks his
cell phone.

On the sidewalk inches away from him, a young homeless
couple sits on a thin, yellow towel. The bloodshot guy holds a
handwritten cardboard sign that says, "Anything Helps."

The young woman has blond pigtails and a scruffy white
puppy on her lap.

People pause to pet the puppy and drop dollar bills or
change on the towel before taking their places behind Mark.

Mark ignores the couple and the dog.

The line of people inches forward.

What could they be serving that makes this place so
popular?

Mark checks his watch, stands on tiptoes and looks up and
down Magnolia Boulevard with exaggerated, self-important
impatience.

A maître d' in leather pants admits a woman with blue dreadlocks and her two male friends into the tiny restaurant.

The line of hopeful diners advances.

Then three young women are allowed inside.

Mark exhales an exasperated breath through his mouth and steps forward.

Suddenly a pasty-looking man in a plaid shirt and khakis and carrying a backpack appears on the corner across the street and jaywalks across Magnolia—stopping traffic—and straight toward Mark. With each heavy footfall his heavy backpack jostles and smacks his wide and fleshy back.

"I'm so sorry, Mark," the man puffs. "How long have you been waiting?"

"Way too long, Joshua," Mark says. "Because of you I'm going to be late for a very, very important meeting. Over the hill."

Mark lets the news of his important appointment on the Westside sink into Joshua's consciousness, then adds, "In Century City."

"The food here is amazing," Joshua says. "Jonathan Gold went crazy for the Indonesian ayam goring breakfast burrito. I think you'll find that it's completely worth the wait."

"I think I won't," Mark says. "I don't give a fuck about the food in this dump." Mark waves his hand to indicate the restaurant, the street it's on, and the world, and the planet that supports them all. "Do you understand? I should never have agreed to a Valley meeting in the first place. Ever. Especially after you sold me such complete shit last week."

"What? You didn't like it?" Joshua says though he's just heard that Mark didn't like it.

By now Mark and Joshua have shuffled slowly forward until they occupy a place in the front half of the line.

"Shit. Utter and complete, total and absolute shit." Mark says. "Which you already knew when you delivered it, asshole."

Joshua reddens from his neck up to his eyebrows. "Gee. I'm sorry you feel that way, Mark. It was supposed to be the best.

Beautiful. Amazing. Awesome. And you're such a special customer. I wanted this to be my treat."

Mark shifts his weight from the ball of one foot to the ball of the other, and steps out of the line toward the curb. His eyes are slits—maybe from the bright whitish light coming from the cloud entombing the sun—or maybe because he's pissed or hung over from last night's festivities with the little—literally—woman. "I don't patronize the so-called 'exclusive' dispensary where you work because I want to smoke shit like the shit you sold me last week. I expect a complete refund and a replacement—with the additional item we discussed—delivered this afternoon."

89.

"I'm so dead." —Derek Farrell

Joshua—his cheeks reversing from crimson to white—watches as my shit brother vanishes around the corner of Lankershim and Magnolia and then he sighs.

Joshua relinquishes his place in line and walks to the traffic light at Blakeslee, waits for the green and crosses quickly. I follow him into the parking structure on the east side, and then to the second floor where he gets inside a blue Subaru.

Once inside his vehicle, Joshua doesn't start the car. He removes a cell phone from his pocket and taps out a text message—

"Need to see u"

Joshua waits, staring at the concrete wall next to his car until the phone chimes.

The green bubble on Joshua's cell phone's screen says, "busy"

Joshua types, "problem for real"

"I fuck w me," the bubble replies.

"not," Joshua insists, "no way"

"K," the phone says and then goes black.

90.

"Death is the end of every worldly pain." —Chaucer

I'm with Joshua as he makes the quick drive from NoHo to Ventura Boulevard in Studio City, and then to a small strip mall that houses a doggy daycare, a nail salon, a tanning salon, a falafel shop and a marijuana dispensary.

The pot shop has valet parking and an arty neon sign above the entrance that says "Kannibliss" over a green neon plus symbol.

The green-vested valet nods as Joshua parks the Subaru in a handicapped-only space and trots past the ostentatiously armed and heavily muscled security guard to a frosted green-tinted glass door.

I expect a head shop like the ones I remember on Fairfax and Sunset when I was young—but this is a goddamned boutique—all bleached hardwood, soft leather sofas, mood lighting and sleek glass and chrome displays—set up exactly like the jewelry stores and the makeup boutiques where my ex-wives bought shockingly expensive creams with names that had words like "Swiss," "pearl," "youth," "maximum," "refresh," "vitality," "serenity" and "serum" in them.

Here the products encased in glass are called "Pink Thunder," "Space Goat," "Green Dream," "Sour Spirit," "Killer Kush," "Thai Elephant," and "Velvet Midnight." There are hundreds of cannabis varieties, and also pot-infused candies, oils, tinctures, Vape pens, lotions, a small raw juice bar and an assortment of pipes.

I move with Joshua past the receptionist—a slender young

woman with white blond hair and frosty white lipstick—then past one of the display cases to a door.

Joshua knocks and enters a windowless back office. There's a huge safe in the corner and an over-muscled middle-aged man with a thick silver nose ring sitting behind a desk and entering a series of numbers on a calculator.

"This better be good," the man says to Joshua as he stops his work. He has an accent. Maybe Russian. "I don't like to see you here."

"I know, Dmitri," Joshua says. "I've got a problem with that prick Mark Stone."

"What is it now?"

"He says the Thai sativa was shit. Wants a replacement with his regular delivery today. That 'shit' was four hundred bucks a gram."

"He's a fucking asshole. But he's a very good customer— stupid and greedy." Dmitri stands up and I see that his green, too-tight t-shirt says "High As Fuck" printed in curly white letters. "I've got something you can give him. It's crap, but he'll never know the difference."

Dmitri puts a black linen sport coat on over his t-shirt and opens the door to the front of the pot boutique. Joshua follows him past the blonde to the back of the display cases. Dmitri removes a large glass canister labeled "Monkey Wrench, $50 per gram, THC 17.0%, CBD 0.16%," removes and weighs two grams of the sponge-like buds, drops them in a glass jar with a stylish Kannibliss label with a green cross on it, picks up a marker and writes, "Suzy Creamcheese!, Denver, 100% Organic," and puts the jar in a white paper bag.

"Now," Dmitri says as he hands Joshua the bag, "fuck off."

91.

"You should have died when I killed you." —John le Carré

Joshua puts the Kannibliss bag in the trunk of the Subaru, nods at the pot shop valet and drives east on Ventura Boulevard to the Hollywood freeway where he directs the Subaru into heavy morning traffic.

His face grim, he switches the car radio from the FM rock station to an all news, all traffic AM station that updates the gridlock every seven minutes.

Mattress in center lane.

Overturned van on the 405 South.

Dog running through traffic on the Golden State Freeway.

Dog.

Hearing that word intensifies my feeling of remoteness—and my desolation.

Perhaps Rose's presence was always meant to be temporary and I just didn't realize it.

Perhaps I got this whole death thing wrong.

It's about an hour after he left the pot dispensary when Joshua parks the Subaru on East Ninth Street downtown.

The storefronts offer a rainbow of textiles on sale in Spanish and in English for ninety-nine cents a yard—many bolts of neon orange and black cloth on sale for Halloween.

I drift behind the backpack as Joshua strides toward a Starbucks at the corner of Ninth—and now I see it—why am I surprised?—La Moda Street.

Joshua enters the coffee shop where youngish people with laptop computers occupy most of the chairs in this Starbucks as they do every other Starbucks on the planet.

A man with white hair—also with a laptop—intently types a few words and then stares thoughtfully at the screen.

Memoir?

Expose?

Elderporn?

A middle-aged woman in a long skirt and boots stares at the surface of her cell and masticates a scone in slow motion.

Which one of these people is Joshua's/Dmitri's cocaine supplier?

I guess I was expecting a drug lab full of heavily tattooed men with five o'clock shadows who look like movie criminals.

Or a drug den.

Whatever the hell that is.

Joshua joins the in line of young men who all look like him and inches past the display of breakfast sandwiches, muffins, juice, Halloween cookies and scones and or stares at the chalkboard on the wall advertising Fall Flavors.

When it's finally his turn Joshua orders a Venti Pumpkin Spice Latte with an extra shot and a chocolate chip scone. He pays with cash from his wallet, and doesn't leave a tip.

The barista asks his name.

"Justin," Joshua says succinctly. "J. U.S.T.I. N."

92.

"When people die, they cannot be replaced." —Oliver Sacks

Joshua carries his scone and mega-latte outside and strides toward La Moda Street.

He takes a dainty bite of the scone, chews it thoughtfully, sips the coffee, and then does something strange—

He stops to adjust the cup so that "JUSTIN" faces outward.

Joshua proceeds along the crowded sidewalk displays of clothing, luggage, handbags, toys, shoes and Halloween costumes and makeup, novelty contact lenses, and glances over his shoulder through me—at the shoppers milling around behind him—then ducks under a display of piñatas into the tiny, narrow shop Mateo and the dwarf visited before.

I am right behind his backpack as Joshua steps to the rear of the store.

A lanky young woman with short, spiked hair and wearing tight and strategically torn and faded jeans and a pink hoodie has replaced Sylvia on the stool by the cash register.

The woman becomes aware of Joshua and stares—not at his face—but at the coffee cup.

She slides so quickly off the stool that she drops her magazine.

That's when I see a hazy reddish shape suspended about a foot off the floor near some boxes covered by a large, pink towel.

93.

"…death is death." —Toko

Because I drift behind the opaque and animate Joshua/Justin—I see Rose before she realizes that I'm here.

The woman with spiked hair bends down to pick up her magazine—revealing black roots and pale scalp—then steps to a display shelf stuffed with plastic Halloween pumpkins and ghost masks at the back of the shop—he has no fucking clue that a large, mute poltergeist has entered the shop with him.

Rose doesn't know, either—I could call her name—but I wait for Rose to notice that I'm here.

Rose's sad face is tilted—and her expressive eyes—the whites thin half-moons edging the murky pupils—are on the towel—fully engaged by whatever it obscures.

Will Rose be glad to see me?

She lived her short life in solitude.

So why shouldn't she experience her death in private and dedicated to her own thoughts?

Her own preoccupations?

I'm sure I felt her absence more keenly than she felt mine.

Suddenly Rose turns—

Raising an eyebrow in recognition—she glides toward me—tail wagging—mouth open—

I move close to her sweet face and her gaunt, familiar form.

94.

"...life well used brings happy death." —Leonardo DaVinci

Joshua places his cup of coffee on the floor and as the woman tugs the shelf away from the wall a few inches to reveal—the way things are going why didn't I guess?—a door hidden behind it which she opens with a key she keeps in her pocket.

She watches Joshua as he puts on his backpack, picks up the coffee cup, open door open and steps into a shadowy landing.

I'm about to follow—but Rose bestows a long, backward look at that pink towel, then turns to me and blinks.

"Let's see where he goes and then I'll look."

Her eyes widen.

"I will. I promise."

Rose dissolves like reddish smoke into the wall.

I follow her through, then waft up a dark, steep, narrow stairway to a second-floor landing that ends at a battered, heavy steel door.

Rose is behind Joshua as he raps the door with one hand and holds the cup in the other.

The knock produces a low murmur inside, then the scrape of a deadbolt sliding free.

The inner door opens enough to produce a vertical bar of gray light and to reveal part of a human silhouette.

"Justin," Joshua says to the shape beyond the screen. He holds the coffee cup close to the security door so the shape can see it.

The figure leans toward the screen, then calls "Justeen" to someone inside who says, "Si."

After a few seconds, the door is unlocked, and an inner door opens.

Joshua steps inside and Rose and I float after him.

95.

"Most people's deaths are a sham. There's nothing left to die…" —Charles Bukowski

Jesus.

It looks like a goddamned piñata factory exploded in here—clowns with gaping holes in their backs, swollen soccer balls and footballs, pink and blue dinosaurs, cross-eyed princesses with orange paper hair, white and purple elephants with abbreviated trunks, short-limbed Spidermen, shell-shocked Winnie the Poohs, stars and suns belching papier-mâché streamers and Halloween pumpkins with black eyes and black Os for mouths, and amputated piñata parts are scattered about the small space.

Joshua raises his arms and allows the man who opened the door—a goateed guy in his late twenties or early thirties wearing a white t-shirt and loose plaid shorts and carrying a thick handgun in a holster—to remove his backpack and to pat him down.

Among the piles of piñatas, a large cardboard movers' box is set up like a work table.

Three guys—also bearded, wearing baggy shorts, white t-shirts and carrying guns—is this a uniform of some kind?—stand around the box and fill small baggies with white powder they scoop out of a foot-long duct-tape-gray plastic package and weigh on small digital scales. Then another guy twists the baggies shut, stuffs them inside a piñata and seals the opening with glue and colored paper.

There's a pile of stuffed and sealed piñatas on the floor next to him.

Rose looks at the men, the white powder, the bags, the piñatas and angles her head at me.

"It's a drug den," I say, "and it's full of fucking party goods."

96.

"What is born will die. What has been gathered will be dispersed. What has been accumulated will be exhausted."
—Sogyal Rinpoche

The armed piñata guy finishes Joshua's pat-down, removes the wallet from Joshua's pocket, unzips the backpack, kicks a piñata out of the way and dumps the backpack's contents on the floor—

A black laptop.

An iPod with tangled earbuds still attached.

A crimson and gold USC sweatshirt and sweatpants.

About a dozen small black plastic canisters.

Some goldenrod yellow plastic pill bottles with white screw-on tops.

And a thick gun with a short handle.

Joshua shrugs.

The man picks up the gun and pockets it, then nods toward the back.

Rose and I are right above Joshua as he steps carefully through the clutter and into a tiny, doorless kitchenette.

Well, look who's here—

Like trolls doing an inventory of stolen treasure in a demented fairy tale—Mateo separates piles of cash into neat stacks of twenties and hundreds which the dwarf—sitting on a stool so he can comfortably reach the egg yolk-yellow Formica countertop—secures into tight bundles—snap, snap, snap—with thick rubber bands.

Joshua ogles the cash and waits for Mateo or the dwarf to speak.

Without looking up or interrupting his work, Mateo says,

"Justeen."

Joshua keeps his pale eyes on the money. "I'm sorry to bother you, Mateo. I have a problem with one of my—one of our—primo customers. And he's expecting a delivery in about an hour."

"Cuánto cuesta?" Mateo says.

"Ten grams," Joshua says, careful to not enter the kitchenette. "Bolivian."

"Who the fuck for?" the dwarf's voice reverberates from inside his barrel chest.

"A rich Beverly Hills asswipe. A total douche."

"Diez gramos for the douche." Mateo pronounces "douche" with an extra syllable at the end as in "touché." "Mil dolares."

Mateo carefully straightens a pile of hundreds and attacks another pile of bills.

But the dwarf stops bundling, climbs off the battered metal kitchen stool, and moves—Justin trailing him—to the cardboard work surface where the men are doing their weighing, packaging and piñata-stuffing.

The dwarf takes ten small baggies and carries them to the pile of Joshua's belongings on the floor next to the backpack.

The dwarf drops the baggies on the backpack, picks up Justin's wallet and removes hundred-dollar bills one at a time. "Uno, dos, tres, cuatro, cinco, seis, siete, ocho, nueve, diez, once, doce y trece."

Justin seems about to say something about the extra hundreds, but stops himself.

Without a word the dwarf folds the hundred-dollar bills into his pants pocket, receives Joshua's gun from the guy who took it, unloads it, drops it on the backpack, then steps around the piñata piles back into the kitchenette.

Just as silently Joshua returns his belongings to his backpack—and waits for one of the quartet of holstered, bearded men in mirrored sunglasses to unlock the security door and let him the hell out.

97.

"Death is the enemy. But the enemy has superior forces. Eventually, it wins." —Atul Gawande

At the bottom of the stairs Joshua taps at the door to the La Moda Street shop.

There's the scrape of the shelf being pushed away from the wall.

The door opens.

Joshua nods to the woman in the pink hoodie, then steps quickly through the shop and joins the throng of shoppers on La Moda Street.

I am about to follow him when Rose returns to the pink towel in the corner and looks at me—serious and expectant.

Joshua is already out there on the street—If I don't go now, I might lose him.

But I glide to rear of the store, approach the towel and then float right through it.

98.

"By daily dying, I have come to be." —Theodore Roethke

The towel obscures two chicken wire cages, one stacked on top of the other.

I move through the wire of the top one to get a better view—

When my eyes adjust to the darkness I make out pairs of tiny, gleaming terrified eyes.

Fuck.

These are birds.

Parrots maybe—wrapped tightly in brown paper or cardboard tubes—their beaks taped shut.

99.

"You will be dead soon enough." —Ernest Hemingway

Why are they so quiet?

Fear?

Darkness?

Are the birds drugged?

How long can they survive like this?

I ask myself these miserable questions as Rose and I locate Joshua sidling among the bargain hunters searching and for Halloween costumes, masks and toys on La Moda Street.

If she could—I'm sure that Rose would tell me everything I want to know—

How the birds were smuggled here.

Where they came from.

How they feel.

Well I can fucking guess how they feel—but animals share something pure and more profound than language— illustrated by the way Rose returns to the pink towel before we leave the shop—lowering her head in farewell to the captive birds before returning to my side.

Joshua finally stops at a shop down the block and buys a light black jacket from the sidewalk display.

He walks on—ditching the thin white plastic shopping bag that held the jacket.

The bag swells with a sudden gust and joins Rose and me in the air above the street for a long, silent moment.

Joshua stops, takes off his backpack, puts on the jacket, zips it closed, and then puts his backpack on again and crosses the street.

He buys a dull army green wool hat and a pair of dark sunglasses from a vendor standing under a faded umbrella.

As he walks Joshua puts on the hat and glasses and crosses the street again.

Why would Joshua bother to change his appearance when he's going to make a delivery to my shit brother, a man he knows and who knows him?

Joshua lied to Mateo and to the dwarf.

Not just about his name.

He lied about much more than that.

Where is he really going?

100.

"Death makes angels of us all…" —Jim Morrison

Justin reaches the end of La Moda Street, then trots to his car on East Ninth Street.

Once inside he puts the backpack on the floor of the passenger seat and drives—not toward the freeway and my shit brother's office on the west side—but around the block and back toward La Moda Street—then a long block with one fabric shop after another.

Joshua slows and parks, puts money in the meter, opens his trunk, and puts his backpack inside. He then locks the trunk and—hands in pockets and head down—walks.

As Rose and I float past the shops—roll after bright roll of cloth spilling fabric onto the sidewalk—I notice that the light has darkened like maple syrup from amber to ochre—what time does Mark expect the delivery?

Justin turns into an alley parallel to La Moda Street.

He jogs past Dumpsters and shuttered back entrances spray-painted with red Gordo Locos tags.

He stops and pulls his wool cap low, glances over his shoulder—maybe gauging where he is—then up at the fire escapes and blank second-story windows.

101.

"Sleep after toil, port after stormy seas, Ease after war, death after life does greatly please." —Edmund Spenser

What Rose and I see in the alley behind La Moda Street—
A man urinating.
A sparrow bathing in a dirty puddle.
An old woman with a burrito.
A rat.
The urinator is merely passing through.
Ditto for the sparrow.
The old woman is here on purpose.
She wears black socks, yellow faux fur bedroom slippers, a green floral house dress and a heavy parka and pulls a shopping cart loaded with scavenged soda cans and plastic bottles.
The woman removes a wax-paper wrapped package from her parka's pocket, unfolds the paper as if what's inside is extremely fragile—the burrito—groans as she bends and places it near one of the Dumpsters.
A pregnant rat scurries from beneath a Dumpster and gnaws off one of the burrito's corners.
The woman and Rose watch entranced as the rat holds the burrito bit with its tiny pink hands and chews as if it were a miniature ear of corn.
The rodent's feast ends when a dusty white van with painted with flames, balloons and sloping red letters that say "Fiesta Piñata's" enters the alley.
Joshua ducks into a doorway as van bounces over potholes and stops.

The rat retreats below the Dumpster.

The old woman pulls her cart out of the alley and back onto the street.

The old woman gone, the van driver taps the horn twice, then gets out of the van and opens the back doors.

The driver is dressed in dark work pants and a denim shirt and wears a dark blue baseball cap.

I kept expecting one of the first-floor shutters to be rolled up in response to the honks—but nothing happens.

The doors stay closed.

Then a second-floor window is pushed open, and a man crawls out of it onto the narrow fire escape.

The man on the fire escape has a beard and wears mirrored sunglasses, plaid shorts, a white t-shirt.

102.

"I love my wife. My wife is dead." —Richard Feynman

It's the drug-bagging piñata guy who works for Mateo and the dwarf.

Or one of the piñata guys.

He reaches into the window and pulls out a lumpy trash black bag, then dangles it over the side of the fire escape.

The man in workpants nods to the guy on the fire escape.

Piñata guy on the fire escape releases the bag.

The man in workpants catches it in both hands without much effort—so the bag can't be very heavy—and lifts the bag into the van.

More bags are pushed through the window and dropped from the fire escape and placed inside the van.

How many are in there? A dozen? Fifteen?

As the man shuts the van's back doors, Joshua sprints down the alley and around the corner to his car.

103.   ´

"One always dies too soon—or too late." —Jean Paul Sartre

His engine running, Joshua waits for the van to exit the alley, then follows two car-lengths behind Fiesta Piñata's to Cesar Chavez and then from Cesar Chavez Boulevard to where it becomes Sunset and then all the way on Sunset to Hilgard Avenue in Westwood.

The traffic is horrific—the drivers sociopathic—just the usual L.A. rush hour demented dystopian hellscape.

Helmet-less motorcyclists performing lane splits.

Homicidal bicyclists.

I did mention that an enraged bicyclist shot me, right? Well if I didn't, I am mentioning it now.

I have to admit that Joshua is a good driver.

He maneuvers around the plodding, erratic and jaywalking homeless, outwits cyclists and tailgaters—his hands on the steering wheel at ten and two—exactly as I remember being taught in Drivers' Ed.—his eyes on the back of the piñata van at all times.

When the van finally turns into the driveway of a large colonial on Hilgard, Joshua parks in a permit-only spot, releases his death-grip on the wheel and punches a number into his cell phone.

"Mr. Stone? It's Joshua. I'm really sorry the delivery is late, but I'm stuck in traffic on the Harbor Freeway."

Joshua unconsciously nods his head as he listens to the succession of abusive things my shit brother says to him.

Then Joshua smirks. "Uh huh. Sure, Mr. Stone," he says, adopting an ingratiating and weirdly formal tone.

What was it Emily Dickinson said about formality and great pain?

Well my shit brother Mark Stone is one great fucking pain—in the ass.

"An hour at least," Joshua says, his eyes on the van a few houses away. "Maybe More. Yes. Yes. Thank you, sir."

104.

> "Should someone ask
> where Sokan went,
> just say,
> 'He had some business
> in the other world.'" —Yamazaki Sokan

Joshua jabs an icon on his cell phone screen and ends the call. "Fuck you, you fucking douche," Joshua says after the disconnect then gives my shit brother or Westwood or the universe the finger. "A few more days and I won't be making deliveries to asshole douche asswipes like you ever again."

Joshua looks back at the van.

The driver gets out, goes to the back, and opens the doors.

A man I didn't know was in the back jumps out, then unloads two of the lumpy bags and a crude blue dinosaur helium piñata on a string.

The man from inside the van wears the plaid shorts, white t-shirt, shades outfit that I've discovered is so popular among those who labor in the bustling piñata industry.

Rose and I drift above the man with the bags and the driver with the dinosaur piñata as they proceed up the walkway to the front of the house.

A Mylar dinosaur balloons secured to an ornate white iron mailbox on the front porch bob in the wind and startle Rose, who darts behind me.

The man with the piñata knocks on the front door on which a cardboard dinosaur cutout is taped with a handwritten sign that says, "Happy Birthday Andrew!"

105.

"The death of a beautiful woman, is unquestionably the most poetical topic in the world." —Edgar Allan Poe

A slim woman with her black hair twisted in an artfully messy bun opens the door. The wide, deep foyer behind her through which a golden beam of sunlight streams from a skylight looks like a Vermeer.

"Piñata delivery," the guy waves the dinosaur on his string to demonstrate the nature of their visit.

Piñatas? You don't fucking say.

The woman nods them in and Rose and I follow into a large mirrored foyer filled with white orchids—each stalk straining under the weight of its effusive flowers, their blooming precisely peaked in a hot house somewhere—in little terra cotta pots on little oriental tables—a rustic display that just screams florist.

Or maybe florists.

I know.

This is exactly the kind of ostentatious faux-French-fucking-farmhouse, over-the-top wannabe elegant display my ex-fucking wives favored—then dumped the orchids in the garbage the moment one petal faded or fell—and then ordered the delivery of replacement plants so perfect that they looked fake.

I can't tell if the woman knows the piñata guys or not as she leads them along a hallway from which I can see a massive living room—all beams, white couches, antiques and oil paintings of gleaming horses with their tails lifted the air as if their asses have just been smacked—through a large butler's pantry into a huge open kitchen filled with people in black aprons who must be caterers, women who look like housekeepers and a few women in dressy, casual outfits.

"The piñata people are here."

And the ghosts.

One of the fancy, dressy women—this one in skinny jeans, scary-pointy high heels, and a long, soft orange sweater, frizzy red hair and wide green eyes—steps to the guy with the dinosaur piñata in his hand.

"It's not as big as I thought it would be," she says doubtfully. "Will this accommodate twenty children? How much candy— exactly—will this piñata hold?"

The piñata man says, "He's big, Missus. He's very big. He holds five to seven pounds."

The woman twirls one of her long gold earrings in the shape of a fish—the tail is jointed and the eyes are rubies—while she considers this. "What do you think, Karen? You're the expert party planner. Will this piñata do?"

A woman with thick dark hair and wise, dark eyes stops filling party favor bags with shredded blue paper and little toys and warily approaches the piñata as if it is alive and venomous and might spew its poison from hidden orifices at any moment.

She studies the paper figure, then touches the dinosaur's bloated abdomen gingerly as if poking too hard might bring the enraged paper lizard to life.

"I think we can make it work." She turns to a young man with his hair in a bun who is piping frosting stars on a massive dinosaur birthday cake. "Daniel, make sure to use the small stuff, but no lollipops or hard candies. We don't want any choking hazards and we want to maximize the number of candies inside."

"Okay," Daniel says. "I think we have enough fruit leathers and stuff like that."

The crisis over, Karen sighs, "Thank God. I hate to admit it, but I have no Piñata Plan B."

Now that Karen has approved of it, scary-heels woman

takes possession of the papier-mâché dinosaur and carries it to a long table under a large window covered with wide plantation shutters.

The man who had the piñata says, "And Mr. Andre's order? Is Mr. Andre here?"

"I don't know why he had to do this today of all days," the woman complains—then for the benefit of the caterers and Karen and others she's assembled to honor the anniversary of the birth of the invisible Andrew, "Why doesn't my husband realize that I have a massive party to organize and guests arriving in an hour and a half?"

Karen agrees, "Husbands just don't get how much work goes into a birthday party. Believe me, I know."

Sweater woman laughs then says to the piñata guy, "Remind me. What order?"

"The company Halloween party order," the man says. "Mr. Andre said to bring it to the house."

The man lifts the large lumpy black bag to green eye level.

"Well that thing can't stay in here." She lifts a French-manicured finger to indicate the incredibly enormous kitchen and then to point her diamond-ringed index finger at the large, unsightly bag. "It has to go to my husband's office immediately. But be sure to knock first. He hates being disturbed when he's working."

The way they say "husbands," it's hate at first sight with this fucking woman.

And the cake.

And the frosting.

And the goddamn party favors.

And the birthday boy Andrew and the nanny who must be supervising him right now—wherever the hell he is.

The woman and her kitchen and the horse's ass oil paintings and the people she's hired to work for her all take me right back to my massively humiliating, delusional, masochistic relationship mistakes—otherwise known as my failed, grotesque and loveless marriages.

I need out of this place.
I need Grace.

106.

"Those who live, live off the dead." —Antonin Artaud

"Let's go, Rosie."

One of Rose's ears lifts to indicate that she's heard me.

But Rose isn't moving toward the street and away from this place.

Not yet.

She floats above the piñata guys as they exit the kitchen—then through a spacious laundry room filled with straw baskets and more goddamn orchids, then behind the men through a distressed oak door.

These men know their way around.

They know where the office is.

Mr. Andre—whoever he is—it's clear that they work for him.

Rose travels silently above the men—through jagged branches of a mature sycamore that stoops above tables covered with blue cloths arranged at artful intervals on a sweeping lawn.

On each blue table, more metallic dinosaur balloons struggle to break free of the foil-wrapped weights to which they've been tethered by the party planner.

Crepe paper streamers—blue of course—shiver in what must be a refreshing breeze.

Beyond the grass, the trees, and the tables, there is a clay tennis court, a four-or five-car garage and beyond that a guesthouse or office.

The men follow an artfully curving flagstone path.

Someone has forced a thorny climbing white rose bush to grow inside a narrow trellis over the guesthouse door.

The man holding the bag knocks smartly on the door's lacquered surface.

"Who's there?" a male voice says from the other side.

"Party delivery," the other man says. "For Mr. Andre."

I wonder what it is that Mr. Andre does.

Or why Rose is interested.

Maybe it is the kid.

The birthday boy Andrew.

Rose melts through the twisted roses, the wall, and into the guesthouse.

I arrive inside as the Asian men I saw at Beverly Hills Dreaming admits the piñata guys into an entryway that widens into a large, wood-paneled room.

More paintings of shiny horse's asses, tails up—orange sweater or her decorator must have gotten quite a deal on these shitful things.

On one wall a bar. Cut crystal decanters glisten, their interiors full of brown and golden liquids.

Rose glides past the Asian man, the piñata men—the paintings, the bar, above the overstuffed leather couches and chairs and the gleaming tables supporting those green glass lamps lawyers always have—to a closed door and through it into another large room.

I hear her deep growl just as I enter.

Rose's eyes are wide and wild.

Andreas.

He stands behind a huge carved wooden partner's desk, a copy of the Resolute in the Oval Office, I think. But the gleaming surface of this desk is littered with little plastic baggies that contain something powdery and white—

And a huge teddy bear piñata whose distended belly Andreas is gutting with a mother of pearl-handled serrated knife.

107.

"We might as well die as to go on living like this." —Charlie Chaplin

What a putz I am—

Mr. Andre is Andreas from Beverly Hills Dreaming.

The schlock shop on La Moda Street and the coke operation are his—with a little help from the Gordo Locos.

Of fucking course.

And Hope found out—I'm not sure how—yet—but I'm sure she did.

And Andreas knew she knew.

So Hope decided to die—before they could kill her—or hurt Grace.

108.

"Let aeroplanes circle moaning overhead
Scribbling on the sky the message 'He is Dead'." —W.H.
Auden

Low clouds, the colors of pewter and tarnished silver seem to hold a heavy darkness and weigh the sky down.

Rose and I watch Grace get out of a car.

It's a shiny electric blue Kia with a pink and white Lyft sign on the dashboard—stopped in one of the visitor parking spaces at the North Hollywood Police Station.

Grace looks thin in a long, loose black sweater and black pants.

I scan Burbank Boulevard in both directions.

If Grace has a police escort or undercover protection I don't see it—unless the woman with lip, cheek and nose piercings and the half-shaved, half-spiked hair who drove Grace here is a plainclothes officer masquerading as a Lyft driver.

The driver stays in the car and looks at her cell phone. She does not move her heavily thickly mascaraed eyes from the screen or seem interested in watching Grace's deliberate approach to the station entrance.

Does Grace know that she is in the exact place where her sister died?

A black and white enters the lot and Grace retreats a few paces to give it room to enter the police lot in the back.

Grace returns to the middle of the driveway.

She drops to her knees and presses her delicate, sensitive hands flat on the pavement as if to detect some movement or vibration coming from deep in the earth below.

Yeah.

Grace knows.

109.

"'It is required of every man,' the ghost returned, 'that the spirit within him should walk abroad among his fellow-men…'" —Charles Dickens

They've repaired the glass block walls and glass entry doors.

A visitor would never know that not so long ago a young woman shot up the place.

Rose drifts near Grace as she tells the officer on duty in the department lobby—a man with an extremely large, square head and a bright ginger moustache—that she has an appointment to see Officer Ventresca.

"Your name, Miss?"

Grace gives her name.

If he connects this Morgan to the Morgan whom his colleagues shot to death in perfect demonstration of defensive overkill, he doesn't betray it.

The officer lifts the receiver on a telephone behind the front desk. "Miss Morgan is here," he says to someone at the other end.

After a moment the door in the back opens and Officer Ventresca steps to the front desk and waves Grace into area in the back. "Miss Morgan. Good to see you again. Thanks for coming in."

Grace—eschewer of small talk and hater of bullshit—and Rose wordlessly follow Officer Ventresca to a cubicle where Officer Ang waits in one of two straight-backed chairs across from a very neat desk covered with foot-high stacks of files and white plastic notebooks with post-it notes in rainbow colors peeking from among their pages.

"Coffee?" Officer Ang asks. "It's not as good as Peet's or

Coffee Bean, but it's definitely caffeinated. And someone from the night shift bought in some bear claws from DuPar's. They're good. Totally worth the calories."

"No thanks," Grace says quickly and sits—her back very straight, her knees touching.

She is definitely thin. And pale.

Rose places herself above Grace's head—tense, eyes downcast—mimicking Grace's mood and attitude.

Officer Ang glances at Officer Ventresca and then says, "Thanks again for coming in, Ms. Morgan. Officer Ang and I thought it would be better if we could go over things in person."

Grace nods, but doesn't help him along.

"I want to assure you that we have devoted all resources available to the investigation of your sister's tragic death," Ventresca offers.

Grace tilts her head.

"...and to finding the perpetrators of the break-in and vandalism of your residence—and the cemetery shooting."

Rose tilts her head, too but Officer Ventresca has nothing else to say.

Ang speaks slowly and quietly, "We're very sorry to have to tell you this, Ms. Morgan, but we've basically dead-ended on everything." Ang shrugs, "There's nowhere left for us to go. Nothing more to check out."

"What about the graffiti in my condo?"

"Those were investigated," Ang says. "The tags belong to a downtown gang that's been expanding into other parts of the city. But we think the break-in was a mistake. We're sure they thought your condo belonged to someone else."

"Who?"

Officer Ang says, "About six months ago, one of the condos on your floor was sublet to persons engaged in illegal gambling. We think the Gordo Locos may have been targeting those people—not you."

Grace sits straighter—if this is possible—in her seat. "And they shot at me at the cemetery by mistake, too?"

"We don't have any positive i.d.s on the drive-by," Ventresca explains. "Your description was vague. And the officer assigned to you thinks that the shooter was wearing a disguise. The car we Hollywood Division found was clean. Nothing in that incident can be connected to the Gordo Locos—which is why we believe it was a random shooting, Ms. Morgan."

"So you're saying I'm just having a streak of really bad luck? My sister arranges to have herself shot to death right outside this building, my condo is trashed and spray-painted with some gang—Locos—insignias, and then someone takes a shot at me when I'm visiting my friend's grave?"

Friend?

Officers Ang and Ventresca are silent.

"But what about that list of people who attended the memorial?"

"Everyone that signed the visitor book was who they said they were," Officer Ang says. "Everybody checked out."

"And the gang? Was Hope involved with them?"

"For reasons of her own, your sister went to great lengths to keep her life private. Secret, even. If she had a connection to the Gordo Locos, we couldn't find it."

"All we can determine is that your sister's tragic death was a suicide," Officer Ventresca says. "She's not the first distressed person to behave in this way, I'm sorry to say. Any gang connection would have to come from another direction."

Officer Ang and Officer Ventresca look meaningfully at Grace now.

Grace flushes, and her dark eyes spark with anger. "Me? You're kidding, right?"

Officer Ang removes a folder from the top of one of the neat stacks on her desk, opens it and removes a photocopy of the *L.A. Times* 'Arts' section article that includes a photo of Grace standing before a brick wall covered with graffiti.

"What about this, Ms. Morgan?" Officer Ang slides the photocopy toward Grace.

I look over Grace's shoulder as she reads.

Rose is still right above Grace's head.

"Morgan Carries On Tradition of Iconic Performance Artist," the headline proclaims, and then, "Grace Morgan's latest series of performance pieces take up where Chris Burden's 'Shoot' left off by locating the artist in physically dangerous, life-threatening contexts that jar and dislocate the viewer…"

"You're saying I arranged the break-in? And for someone to take shots at me? Just because in nineteen seventy-one Chris Burden had someone shoot him?"

"We're saying, Ms. Morgan," Officer Ventresca corrects her, "that we've explored every lead. And this is a lead. Any reasonable person would have to admit that an artist whose work involves staging life-threatening stunts might arrange to have someone take a shot at her. Or to have break-in occur at her residence."

"We've investigated everyone connected to your sister that we could locate," Officer Ang jumps in. "Including you. Just look at that photo, Ms. Morgan and maybe it will refresh your memory."

Grace tilts her eyes toward the paper again.

I look again, too, and then I see it—a large Gordo Loco tag spray-painted on the brick wall behind Grace.

"I never even noticed," Grace says, shocked when she sees the spray-painted design on the wall in the photograph. "I mean this was two years ago. At a gallery downtown. There's graffiti everywhere—you know that. This sign on the wall had no connection to me or my performance."

Officer Ventresca crosses his arms across his chest.

"Ms. Morgan," Officer Ang says, rising from her chair, "if you recall anything—maybe an acquaintance who might be involved in gang-related or illegal activities—or if you think of a detail you overlooked that might be relevant, please call us immediately—day or night. The North Hollywood Division is always here for you."

110.

"Death is a fearful thing." —Shakespeare

Rose has assumed her default Dead Dog position—curled up, head-on-paws, tail tucked under, eyes wide open—a few inches above Grace's right shoulder. She's been this way since Grace left the North Hollywood police station—until now.

Rose lifts her head and blinks, extends her paws, and stiffens as she stares out the driver's side window of the gray Toyota as it moves along La Moda Street.

Then Rose turns her head and levels a significant look at me.

The parrots caged in the La Moda Street shop—I get it.

I haven't forgotten.

"I know, Rosie" I say. "I'm working on it. Trying to figure out a way to help those birds—to set them free—"

Technically true—.

But incomplete.

I have no fucking idea what to do.

As if Rose has read my mind she blinks again and flattens her ears.

She knows.

There is no way I can do much for those parrots right now.

All I can do is promise Rose that I won't give up—

On the birds.

On her.

On Hope.

And I won't give up on Grace—who drives past the Trade Tech campus and—my heart would sink or break if I had a working model—turns into the desolate alley that is Palo

Pinto Street.

Grace drives past 1442—but doesn't slow until she reaches a trio of tall, closed Dumpsters.

She stops the Toyota behind the first Dumpster, and shuts off the engine.

Then she waits.

111.

"Death is better…" —Aeschylus

The bleak day mutes into twilight and after that a soft darkness that smudges the living world's hard edges.

Grace is still here—in the driver's seat observing the entrance to 1442 Palo Pinto Street.

Grace's loose black outfit melts into the dark, her lovely face is lunar in its paleness.

Grace is as languid as Rose—and as silent.

The sky is almost black when a cyclist turns onto the narrow street.

Grace crouches as he rides past the Dumpsters.

The man cycles a few feet past 1442, then halts.

112.

"What men call their understanding, by which they believe they can control the course of time, is the expression of spiritual beings behind." —Rudolph Steiner

As soon as the bicyclist stops, I ease through the car's exterior into the alley.

Rose stays with Grace—but her eyes follow me to the door at 1442.

The figure dismounts and rolls the bike behind a tall stack of wooden pallets. He wears dark clothing—navy-blue or black—sneakers and a hooded jacket—and carries a handled paper grocery bag.

The figure steps from behind the pallets—looks both ways—then walks quickly through me and unlocks the door with a key.

Before I pursue him inside, I look back at Grace.

But she's already out of the car, sprinting toward the door with Rose—ears erect, eyes wide and her feet churning in the air—beside her.

113.

"Death is an evil…" —Sappho

I'm just through the wall when the sound of Grace's fists against the door vibrates through the shadowy, low-ceilinged interior.

The hooded figure seems unsure what to do—ignore the knocking or stop it somehow—but the insistent pounding compels the figure to face the door.

The outdoor security light's reptilian green glow shines through the blinds, revealing the curves of breasts and hips that loose clothing can only partially obscure—

He is a she.

The bicyclist is a woman.

She drops her bag and speaks, "What do you want?"

She doesn't shout, but she's firm. And there's an accent.

"I need to talk to you." Grace says.

Silence.

"I need help. Please. Help me!"

More pounding.

One of the woman's hands is on the battered doorknob—the other unconsciously rises to her forehead and pushes the hood back.

She's thirtyish, with a round face, full lips and thick eyebrows. Her thick, straight dark hair—pulled back in a ponytail—is dyed silver or white at the ends.

Grace shouts again, "Please. Help me!"

The woman unlocks the door.

Grace and Rose pass like puffs of smoke over the threshold and then dissolve into the interior darkness.

114.

"If you fear death, die now!" —Hakuin

The woman shuts the door, then fumbles as she locks it with a key she wears on a string or chain around her neck.

Her hands tremble.

But Grace is unafraid.

She stays where she is near the door.

She does not step toward the woman.

She's still.

I hang in the air near Grace—knowing that I cannot protect her—waiting for what will happen next.

Grace doesn't speak—instead her expression is fierce and questioning.

The woman responds by reaching into her jacket pocket—for a weapon?

No.

A cell phone.

She taps the surface and a blue-white light switches on.

She directs its beam across Grace's black shoes, over her clothes and over her face.

The bright light blackens Grace's hair and bleaches her skin and the silver strands in her dark hair of color.

Grace reminds me of a black and white photo of very young Georgia O'Keefe I saw once in a coffee table book one of my ex-wives bought and never read—defiant.

"Do you live here?" Grace asks.

The woman frowns as if she's solving a math problem in her head. "Nadie—nobody lives here," she says. "People stay."

Grace nods. "My sister was one of those people. May I look around?"

Before the woman can reply, Grace is crossing the room—Rose sailing above her—to the corner mattress where we saw the children sleep.

The air mattress is still there—but no sign of the mother or the kids.

Rose looks at me.

Where are they?

What has happened to them?

I shrug.

"Did anyone come with you here?"

"No. I'm alone," Grace says.

Grace kneels and runs her fingers lightly over the mattress's surface—then hurries into the small bathroom.

Grace pulls the chain on the single-bulb fixture—

Toilet.

Small, stained pedestal sink.

And a round-handled ceramic cup sitting its edge.

It's the Judy Morganthal cup I saw before—decorated with glazed images of two little girls—one with red hair, the other black—dancing among brightly-colored flowers.

115.

"I just don't want to die alone, that's all." —Richard Pryor

"Oh," Grace says—then touches the cup with both hands. "She was here," Grace says.

The woman frowns, then directs the cell phone light on the ceramic mug.

Grace traces the edges of the black-haired figure with her finger. "My mother made this. That's me." She touches the figure with red hair. "That's my sister. Hope."

An intake of breath. "Esperanza?"

"Esperanza?" Grace repeats, and then, "Of course. Hope. Yes, Esperanza Morgan."

The woman looks at the painted figures on the cup again and then at Grace.

"Come," the woman says, nodding for Grace to follow her into the upstairs room.

116.

"Don't expect praise without envy —until you're dead." — Joan Rivers

Rose and I rise through the low ceiling and into the small second floor room.

In the doorway woman waves her hand and says to Grace, "Esperanza stayed here."

Not much has changed in the monastic space—the mattress, the lamp, the table and the folding chair just as I saw them.

But the blanket that was folded neatly on the mattress is gone.

"What was Hope doing?"

The woman doesn't answer or turn on the lamp.

She relies on weird light from the street for illumination as she steps to the mattress, kneels and then lifts on corner few inches from the floor.

She feels around for something underneath—the folded Spanish language newspaper I remember seeing here before.

She gives the newspaper to Grace. "Your sister left this. And the cup. She said not to throw them away."

Grace reads the headline out loud, "La Ciudad: Trabajadores de la Confección se Defienden."

"Workers?" Grace asks, her eyes shining. "Restaurant workers?"

"Trabadores de costura. Garment workers," the woman says. "Piece workers. Pressers. Operadoras—sewing operators. Esperanza helped them."

117.

"But I do nothing upon myself, and yet I am my own executioner." —John Donne

"Drive around," the woman instructs, circling the air with her finger, then pointing to the right at the end of Palo Pinto Street.

She did not give Grace her name, but offered to take Grace to the place where Hope worked.

Grace turns right onto La Moda Street, then—following the woman's instructions—up and down the one-way downtown streets of the fashion district as the woman reflexively consults the rear-view mirror.

Grace approaches La Puebla Street—a street like the others—lined with two and three-story buildings with shuttered-for-the-night first floor shops, many of them spray-painted with Gordo Locos signs.

"Aquí."

Grace makes a left turn.

"Slow," the woman says.

As Grace directs the Toyota sedately forward, I try to see whom or what the woman is looking for. But La Puebla Street is empty except for two stout women—both wearing blue L.A. Dodgers sweatshirts and dark stretch pants—at a bus stop at the corner—and three boys who look about ten years old clattering past on skateboards.

Maybe it's the streetlights broadcasting their honeyed radiance at the deadpan storefronts—or the symmetrical rows of blank windows above them—but I can't shake the feeling that Rose and I and Grace and this nameless woman have migrated inside a dream—

The buildings, the streetlights, the trees, the sidewalks look porous—paper-thin.

The buildings, the street, the sidewalks seem false—like the sets constructed for my father's TV show and the others on the studio back lot among which—when we would visit with my mother, my shit brother and I were urged to get out of his way and "play"—

"Play" among the back lot "New York" brownstones whose steps led to fake painted-on doors with painted doorknobs—or in a depopulated "Mexican" village whose rustic curving street led to a parking lot filled with golf carts—or the "ranch house" where my belligerent, miserable father sang and danced for the cameras.

My shit brother Mark didn't play—he schemed.

And always won.

He didn't play at home.

At school.

And he didn't play with me—not fucking ever.

On the lot he'd chase after me until I collapsed breathless behind the faux Mexican cantina.

Then he'd declare himself the winner of a race I'd never agreed to enter—pronounce me a fat fuck loser—smoke cigarettes pilfered from my mother's purse and then threaten to murder me if I told.

Well here I am—murdered, all right.

Unable to tell.

A dead man with a dead dog.

A dog that—whether hanging around here near Grace—or sharing a dim corner of afterworld with me—

Demonstrates the only thing I'm sure of any more—

Death can't kill love.

118.

"It's a Mr. Death, dear. He's here about the reaping." —
Monty Python

The woman points to the right as Grace approaches the
intersection, then to the right again until Grace has circled the
block one more time.

A man lying on his side has replaced the women at the bus
stop. A very long raincoat protects him against the night's
chill, and his face is covered with a cap.

The skateboarders have moved on.

"Aquí," the woman says after looking over her shoulder one
last time. "Stop here."

Grace parks and locks the car, then walks with the woman
down La Puebla Street past the mute, closed shops to a blank,
numberless steel door painted the color of curdled cream.

The woman presses a silent buzzer painted the same color
as the door.

A window a floor or two above us scrapes open in answer.

Then, after a minute or two, a peephole opens and a voice
says, "Quiene es?"

The woman from Palo Pinto Street says, "La hermana de
Esperanza."

Nothing.

Not another sound until the security door is unlocked.

I follow the woman and Grace into a small vestibule
covered with hideous chipped and shiny brown paint where a
young Latina with a short hair and muscular, heavily tattooed
arms and hands locks the door again with a key secured on a
large metal ring she clips to a belt loop on her jeans.

What's happened to Rose?

I pass through closed security door back out to the sidewalk. There—

Rose is a dusky smudge among the shadows of an emaciated tree—one paw lifted—her eyes on something or someone down the street.

119.

"…with our deaths we give something to those who are left behind…" —Sherwin B. Nuland

Rose journeys above the sidewalk like mist, then slows above the bus bench where the man with the hat on his face sleeps curled up under the long, wrinkled camel-colored raincoat.

"What is it, Rosie?"

Rose lowers her head to indicate the inert, lumpy figure.

The man is a quiet sleeper.

No heavy breathing.

None of the drunken snores that follow a bender.

For Rose's sake I keep looking.

Along the back of the bench are ads for a dentist who promises to "put his patients to sleep," and for a phone sex service advertises busty women in miniskirts and tight, low-cut blouses who are desperate to chat with YOU RIGHT NOW.

"Okay, Rose?" I say, turning away from the sleeping man and drifting back toward Grace.

But Rose's worried bark makes me swivel in the air.

The man is awake, sitting up on the bench, and adjusting his dark baseball cap on his head.

As he removes the raincoat, I see that his short legs don't reach the sidewalk.

120.

"What indeed is finally beautiful except death and love?"
—Walt Whitman

Was the dwarf following Grace all along?

How did I not see him?

Does Mateo have watchers on Palo Pinto Street?

Inside the buildings?

The dwarf shoves the raincoat deep into a full trash bin, hops from the bench down to the sidewalk and marches toward Grace's Toyota, tapping his cell phone as he goes.

"La hermana está aquí," the diminutive basso profundo says and spits. "Calle La Puebla, ese."

The person at the other end—Mateo? Andreas?—says something.

"Ese, no aquí no," the dwarf replies and spits again for emphasis, clicks off the phone and steps purposely along La Puebla Street.

Rose whines when the dwarf slows at the security door through which Grace and the woman entered.

But she quiets when the dwarf turns, crosses the street and jogs around the corner toward La Moda Street.

I pass through the wall and into the vestibule.

Then—fluid as a fish—Rose moves next to me.

"Let's find Grace," I say.

We ascend through a cracked ceiling and a pair of stockinged feet, then through the body of a slender, middle-aged man into what must have once been a large office.

"Respirar," the man exhorts a small group of barefoot people assembled in a small circle around him—ten people

252

maybe—men and women—all with skin the color of honey or tea or coffee with cream.

"Breathe." The man lifts his arms and takes a long, slow breath, holds it and then exhales.

No can do, buddy.

The people—men and women in their twenties, thirties and some older—imitate his actions, their cheeks puffed full of air until he signals its release.

"Tramo," the man says and stretches his arms up and then down to touch his toes.

"Para su circulación que necesita para respirar, estirar," he says. "Las largas horas sentado puede causar coágulos de sangre. Sitting without a break can cause blood clots. Every few hours in the factory, stand up, stretch and breathe."

Rose joins Grace across the room with the woman from Palo Pinto Street and the tattooed woman who let them in. The tattooed woman nods toward wall covered with handmade posters, notices, skeleton cut-outs and signs— "Celebrar el Dia de los Muertos con Los Hilos de la Justicia," and large cloth banner that says "Hilos de Justicia—Threads of Justice" in appliquéd letters cut from a number of colorful fabrics and threads.

"At Hilos de Justicia—Threads of Justice," the woman says, "we educate garment workers about their rights, and we fight sweatshops, and exploitive, unsafe working conditions."

Her practiced delivery indicates that this woman has given this spiel many times, probably to donors—but Grace is transfixed. "Many workers here in the L.A. fashion district," she gestures toward La Puebla Street with a tattooed arm, "work ten to sixteen hour days in deplorable conditions and often do not earn enough to cover rent and food for their children."

I look around.

Along the walls and under the painted windows are a jumble of folding tables, chairs, boxes and shelves filled with papers, books, papers, office supplies and boxes of Halloween decorations.

The blood clot man has turned toward a handmade poster that says, "OSHA," "Salud y seguridad: Tus derechos. Los baños limpios. Aire fresco. La hora del almuerzo."

I know what OSHA is, and understand "health and safety," "rights," "air," and "bathrooms."

"La ley dice que tiene derechos," the man says.

"These workers receive no sick leave," the tattooed woman is saying. "If their child becomes ill and they must stay home, they lose wages. They perform backbreaking labor in crowded, dusty factories that can reach one hundred and ten degrees during the summer. They are often denied bathroom and water breaks. Exploited sexually. Paid pennies for piece work and denied the wages they earn."

"And Hope Morgan? Esperanza?" Grace says. "She was my sister. Can you tell me what she did here?"

"Your sister educated workers about their rights—about federal child care subsidies and the minimum wage. Before she—left us—she said that she was preparing some wage theft cases."

I'll bet one of them was against California Dreaming.

The tattooed woman moves to another topic, "We're planning a visibility event for Dia de las Muertos," she says, leading Grace and the woman from Palo Pinto Street across the room to a table where three women are sewing and assembling bright orange, yellow and purple tissue paper flowers.

121.

"Being
is dying
by loving…" —Tom Clark

Why was the Threads of Justice woman so cagy with Grace?

Why not name the companies Hope was going to sue?

Why didn't she introduce Grace to the workers Hope was going to represent?

Maybe Hope was the cagy one.

She could have kept her plans quiet because revealing them would have been dangerous.

And the dwarf?

How the fuck did he find Grace?

And why didn't he kill her when he could?

Instead, he said "No, not here" to someone—

Andreas?

Mateo?

The silence crushes me.

The cavernous absence of sound—a stillness that's never been disturbed—a vast hush whose lifeless, dim center houses me and Rose.

Rose is near me—her eyes evaluating the nothingness as if there is something there.

And me?

I contemplate Rose's emaciated and elegant form, her small paws—their pads dry and fissured—and then I extend my grayish fingers to scratch her chest.

"Now what, Rosie?"

Rose flips from horizontal to vertical—like an image on an old, black and white television—so that I can scratch her back.

"We can go back to the police station. I'd like to know what Ang and Ventresca are thinking, what they really know—"

Rose's tail swings back and forth once very slowly.

"Or check out Andreas."

Rose tilts her head.

"Or find Grace."

Her pupils enlarge slowly—like a time-lapse movie of a black flower blooming.

"I've been thinking about her. I can't stop thinking about her—"

Rose descends until we're nose to nose—her expression sorrowful, mysterious and purposeful.

"Obviously I know I'm dead," I say. "Fucking done. And I accept that."

Rose lifts one ear.

"But what I feel doesn't end—what happened to me when I was with Grace doesn't stop happening."

Rose doesn't blink—she just stares. Unbreathing. Unmoving.

"Grace always pushed me. Provoked me. Dragged me forward whether I wanted it or not—just the way she's moving me right now."

122.

"For he counteracts the Devil, who is Death, by brisking about the life." —Christopher Smart

Rose yowls—

I'm not sure if she's affirming or protesting what I said.

But her voice accompanies me into the living world—buzzing inside my dead ears, and competing with the clank of hammers on wood bouncing off the cement floor of the raised circular stage in the Olvera Street Plaza.

Rose swoops down near a bearded man—his hair covered with a gray and white bandana.

Shit.

When I said that Grace pushes me forward, I didn't mean this—

It's hipster John himself.

He's with the tattooed woman and some of the people from Threads of Justice—they're constructing what looks like a tall, narrow display shelf and wooden table.

At least John's not wearing his fucking kilt.

He's dressed in ordinary jeans, a gray sweatshirt and work shoes.

I look around.

If he's here, maybe Grace is close.

The large yellow banner installed across the plaza ripples under the pressure of moving air I cannot feel: "Olvera Street Merchants and El Pueblo Historical Association present Dia de los Muertos. Nov. 1 and Nov. 2. Novenario. Oct 30-Nov 2—7 P.M."

Colorful papers with cut-out designs and Christmas lights

crisscross the plaza and the roof.

Other people are building, too—or decorating tables with fruits and vegetables, sugar skulls, paper flowers, candy, cigarettes, paper plates piled high with rice and beans, and framed photographs.

No Grace.

Rose suddenly rises and passes through the elaborate wrought-iron barrier that encircles the elevated stage.

Has she found Grace?

I follow Rose until she pauses above the park across from Union Station.

Shopping carts, collapsed cardboard boxes and the still bodies of sleeping human figures occupy the sloping, trash-littered lawn.

No Grace here.

Rose dips down close to the human forms—then darts toward a police car with flashing lights stopped next to a van parked in a red zone.

It's not the police—it's a Metro sheriff's black and white.

The van's back doors are open—and painted on its side are the words, "Fiesta Piñata's."

123.

"The only thing people really have in common is that they are all going to die." —Bob Dylan

"You can't park here." The female sheriff in a tan shirt and forest green pants nods toward the "No Parking Any Time" sign a foot away from the van, then smirks at the driver, one of the piñata delivery guys I saw at Andreas's house in Westwood.

"Just a second," the driver says. "We're dropping off piñatas for the Dia de Los Muertos and the streets are all blocked."

"The sign doesn't say 'No Parking except for people making deliveries to Olvera Street,'" the sheriff says, her extremely white gapped front teeth gleaming menacingly.

The driver yells to someone in the back of the van, "Darse prisa! Get the bags out fast!"

Rose barks joyfully as a lumpy, sunburned man in a lime green t-shirt and stained khakis—a clear plastic bag stuffed with orange and black piñatas in each red fist—climbs out of the back of the van.

Jesus.

It's the guy we saw handcuffed in the North Hollywood station.

The mad crapper—

I think his name is Goldberg.

"Where'd you get that shirt?" the Metro Sheriff asks, looking Goldberg up and down.

Printed on the shirt is a silhouette of a deer taking a shit on the silhouette of a plant and the caption, "MY FOOD SHITS ON YOUR FOOD."

"A police officer in Van Nuys gave it to me," Goldberg says. "It's supposed to be a joke."

Rose floats happily over Goldberg's head.

The Metro sheriff shows her teeth again. "And that joke is?"

"Well," Goldberg blushes under his sunburn, "The shirt makes fun of vegetarians—which I'm not. Not at all. But the joke is sort of about me in a way because I used to have a shitting problem—but I'm fine now."

The Metro sheriff looks skeptical.

"I found out that I have Celiac disease," Goldberg offers, "Do you know what that is? It means I'm allergic to gluten."

Jesus.

"Well that's dandy news," the Metro sheriff says. "Just don't let me catch you shitting gluten or whatever the fuck around here. Understood?"

"Got it." Goldberg secures his grips on the unwieldy piñata bags, hoists them up, and then zigzags among the sleeping homeless across the park and toward the Plaza.

Rose whines as if to urge me to follow Goldberg.

I shake my head—I want to hear what the piñata guy says.

The van driver shrugs. "My regular guys were busy with other drop-offs. Halloween is a busy time."

I'll bet it is.

There must be a ton of very special piñatas with grown-up surprises tucked inside just waiting to be delivered.

"So you hired him?"

"He was panhandling," The driver explains. "He said some hospital in the Valley dumped him in the park. I thought I'd do him a favor and give him some work."

But the driver can't help himself and embellishes his narrative with an insincere grin, "I guess no good deed goes unpunished, right?"

"I never want to see you, your fucking piñatas, this van or that man anywhere around here again," the Metro sheriff says. "And if he takes a shit within five miles of Union Station, I'll hunt your ass down."

124.

"All the earth is a grave…" —Nahuatl poem Daniel G. Brinton, translator

Darkness doesn't fall—

It snakes along Los Angeles Street, slides across Father Serra Park and swirls

over sleeping figures, trash cans, the assortment of blanket-and-tarp-covered shopping carts parked around the base of the imploring statue of that sick fuck Father Serra.

Rose coasts toward the Plaza, toward glowing bright colors of the string lights—toward the displays, the murmur of voices, toward Goldberg, toward John and—I hope—toward Grace.

Rose makes a circuit above the stage's covered roof, then returns in a graceful descent to John.

The project is complete—a rectangular table with an arched shelf attached—a display that resembles other memorial altars set up around the plaza—some just simple arrangements of candles and flowers on the ground.

I float around the perimeter and look down at the cloth-covered tables decorated with fruit, vegetables and marigolds—

Laden with candles, skull figurines, plastic skeletons, toys, candies, paper plates of rice and beans, packets of cigarettes, unopened cans of beer and photographs of the dead—most the imaged faded or blurred—cracked, wallet-sized school photos of children against fake blue-gray backgrounds—newborns with pink, swollen eyes shut—slim unsmiling young men in military uniforms—tiny, squinting white-haired

261

women and toothless old men.

The Plaza and Olvera Street are filling with people—many extravagantly costumed, their faces painted white and black and red with flowers and skulls, or wearing white skull masks with frozen grins.

I don't see Goldberg or the van driver.

I don't see Grace.

John helps the tattooed woman from Threads of Justice attach the embroidered banner to the railing behind a table loaded with tissue paper flowers, flyers and handmade signs—

Stop Sweatshops!

Los Imigrantes Tambien Tienen Derechos!

Support Workers!

Stop Wage Theft!

Next to the Threads of Justice altar is a small table—maybe a card table—covered with a white cloth.

Unlike the other displays, this table holds only a few objects—

Two tall white glass candles.

A pile of marigolds.

Two photographs in simple black frames—

A faded-to-orange Polaroid picture of Hope in a stiff, white party dress—eyes scrunched closed—her orangey red hair cut short—cheeks puffed out as she blows out the candles on a small birthday cake.

And the other—

A black and white photo of nondescript, pale, overweight man with a rueful smile. The man points down at something out of frame with one hand, and shades his eyes from the unrelenting sun with the other.

125.

"The goal of all life is death." —Sigmund Freud

Shit.

That schmuck in second photo is me.

Or was.

I remember that smoggy, white-hot September day—

Grace insisted on seeing my father's star on the so-called "Hollywood Walk Of Fame"—the one he paid or with a generous "donation" to someone on the chamber of commerce.

I remember the moment—despite my protests—when Grace took the picture.

She was intent.

Serious—as if a photograph of me at that moment really mattered.

And I remember what happened before and what happened after.

The cool, sweet, lingering floral taste of Grace's kiss.

What the hell is Grace doing?

Where the fuck is she?

John tilts the glass candle next to the photograph of Hope and ignites the wick after a few tries with a lighter—then repeats the operation with the candle near mine.

Two weak flames waver inside the glass—making the photographs shimmer.

Rose dips low—her paws sliding through the glass and the uncertain flames—as John taps a number into his cell phone.

"The altar's done. I'm ready. Are you?"

126.

"And when the Earth shall claim your limbs, then shall you truly dance." —Kahlil Gibran

John says something more as he steps toward the tattooed woman from Hilos de Justicia—but I can't hear him.

A company of barefoot native dancers wearing feather headdresses, some with their faces painted like skulls, others carrying bowls of burning incense, drums, and large conch shells, solemnly step along the narrow cobblestone street lined with touristy shops and stalls and enters the Plaza.

Revelers follow the dancers into the Plaza. A man in a serape holding a bouquet of bright tissue paper flowers and a bowl of and burning incense. Mariachis. A skeleton bride and groom. Three young women, their black hair piled high and secured with blood-crimson artificial roses. Skeleton men on stilts, children in brightly embroidered Mexican dresses and wearing death-head masks, people in street clothes holding paper skulls on ribboned sticks.

A young male dancer lifts a conch shell to his mouth and blows—

The world stills as the mournful hollow sound hangs in the air above the Plaza.

Now the rhythmic dancing and drumming resumes as dancers kneel offer and incense to the north, south, east and western reaches of the night sky, scattering marigold petals—sprinkling water on the pavement—summoning the dead.

The dancers spin—the shells on their bare ankles and the beads on their costumes glittering and clattering as if something fragile is shattering.

Rose darts back and forth, barking in alarm.

Oh fuck.

Oh Jesus.

The vaporous dead are assembling above the Plaza—

They drop down as silently and serenely as snowflakes— among the altars erected in their memory—

Their pathetic, shriveled, skinny asses hanging out of hospital gowns—

Their heads bald and their bodies cancer-emaciated—

Fat, middle aged men who kicked in their sleep—their unshaven faces still registering surprise that their hearts attacked—

Jaundiced infants with tubes in their noses.

Old women drowned by the fluid in their own rasping lungs.

Here come the car-crashed and car-smashed—among them misshapen lumps of dead dog flesh that Rose greets solemnly—her tail between her legs.

There a young half-of-his-head-exploded gun suicide wreathes himself around an altar displaying a six-pack of Dos Equis.

Oh fuck.

Here they come.

The wide-eyed suffocated SIDS babies.

Slack-mouthed overdosed teenagers.

Young muscular men in work clothes whose dead heads tilt on broken necks.

And then—arriving at the altar that John built like a moonbeam—here comes Hope.

127.

"Death makes me mad." —Philip K. Dick

Rose rotates and—head down and bashful—tail swinging wildly—sails up to greet her.

"Hope!" I shout—before I can stop myself—as if I'm alive and she's alive and we're long lost friends who just happened to run into each other at a concert—

But Hope—fastidious even in death—and wearing the bloodstained, bullet-holed t-shirt and jeans she wore when she died—recoils.

"What's going on, Charles?" Hope surveys the dancers, the lights, the people, the memorial altars—her curdling gaze lingering on Rose and me.

"Why am I here?"

"I'm not sure," I say, "I have no fucking idea, really—except that you and the others have been honored—and summoned."

"So you summoned me?" she asks—with emphasis on "you."

"No, Not me." I say. "Grace. Look at the altar."

Hope descends to the altar—lowering her head to study her photo and then mine—her copper hair covering her face—the way a hummingbird pauses mid-air to sip flowers—passing through John as he watches the dancers.

"Grace feels really terrible about—what happened, Hope. And I know she blames herself for the estrangement."

Hope lifts head. "It wasn't her fault," she says. "But she can't bring me back. She can't change anything."

"Grace has been trying to find out why you died the way you did. She visited Palo Pinto Street. Went to Threads of Justice—"

Grace's eyes widen. "No, she can't do that, Charles—she has to stay away—"

"—Why, Hope? Tell me. I know that Grace is in danger," I interrupt. "And she and her loser boyfriend—" I look down at John, "don't have a fucking clue."

128.

"No single thing abides; and all things are fucked up." — Philip K. Dick

The dancers pivot in unison.

John steps away from the altar and trots to the Plaza's edge—removing a small, digital camera from his pocket and—facing north—snapping photographs.

I look where John looks—beyond the dancers and the dead above them—scanning the crowd.

Jesus.

Hope's ghost has a twin.

Or this is someone dressed to look like her.

The long hair burns copper in the flickering light—

Black bullet holes and a huge blood-reddish stain obscures the words printed on the front of her t-shirt.

And unlike Hope's, this face glows with bone-white greasepaint—black smears delineating a skull's triangular nose-hole—the cavernous eye sockets—and the wide, gaping mouth.

Shit.

It's Grace.

Rose—confusedly looking back at Hope floating above the altar—darts eagerly toward Grace as she threads her way among the dancers, through clouds of smoldering incense— and travels among the bystanders, until she melts into the shadows of the dim cobblestone pathway.

129.

"It is impossible to experience one's death objectively and still carry a tune." —Woody Allen

Grace—Rose and I and Hope above her—moves past the people pressed among displays of leather sandals, glassine packets of jumping beans, serapes, blown glass, pottery, cheap guitars, Mexican candies, and maracas.

Glancing back toward the Plaza I see John pushing his way through the crowd that journeys solemnly from the Plaza into the narrow passageway.

Grace—in reddish wig and wearing the clothes Hope wore when she died—moves along the worn, reflective cobblestones—pausing only for a crowd that blocks the passageway where it widens to meet Cesar Chavez Boulevard.

Here people jostle each other as they watch women in bright Mexican dresses apply skull face paint to toddlers—

As they cheer the children whacking piñatas with long wooden sticks—piñata pumpkins, skeletons and smiling skull-heads hanging at various heights from the large, gray-trunked olive tree.

When Grace steps around the circular base of the piñata tree, she looks back—her huge black-painted eyes staring right through me and right through Hope—as she searches for John.

"What the fuck does Grace think she is doing?" I say.

"Where did she get my clothes?"

"From the coroner."

"Is this a performance piece?"

"A provocation," I say. "Everything Grace does is meant to

provoke—and now I think she's trying to provoke whoever made you do what you did."

Hope shivers in the air as if she's suddenly very cold. "No," she says. "We have to stop her."

"What the fuck do you think I've been trying to do?" I say. "She can't hear us. She can't see us. She can't touch us. So what the fuck do you suggest?"

Hope is silent as the crowd cheers as a little girl in a pale blue Disney princess costume cracks open a fat pumpkin piñata, candies skittering across the cobblestones.

The children swarm and shove each other as they fight over the confections.

Then clack and clatter of shells and the moan of the conch announce the arrival of the dead-invoking, dead-consecrating procession of dancers.

The drum-pulse quickens.

More onlookers push their way below the piñata tree.

Grace shrinks back as the skeleton-bride in long black mantilla dances flirtatiously toward her—batting her black, oversized spidery eyelashes and waving a fan near Grace's painted face.

Grace spins around—afraid?—and runs.

130.

"Oh, may I join the choir invisible of those immortal dead who live again." —George Eliot

"Where is she?" Hope cries out.

But I've lost Grace.

Rose's eyes are wild.

She paws the air above the living heads nodding in rhythm to the insistent and hypnotic drums—the living eyes shimmering behind expressionless skull masks.

John elbows his way under the piñata tree.

He looks around, confused—where's Grace?—then puts his camera his one pocket and takes his cell phone out of the other.

Rose barks shrilly—her tail straight—and stares toward the Cielto Lindo restaurant on the corner.

I search the faces of the people waiting in line at the restaurant—and then look at the street beyond.

The Fiesta Pinata's van—

It's double-parked and idling at the corner—the back doors open.

Goldberg watches the procession of costumed figures and the dancers from inside the van.

Rose yips.

"What? What is it?" Hope says.

"I can't explain now—" I say. "Something bad."

The skeletons on stilts march around the piñata tree—and Grace reappears right behind them—walking sedately now—giving John time to take photographs.

"Look! Over there."

A short, thick figure—a black and gold skull mask obscuring his wide face and a dark baseball cap on his head—pushes toward Grace, then swiftly extends a thick arm and clasps it around her waist.

Grace's black-painted mouth opens in surprise—

But the dwarf is powerful and fast—he lifts his free hand up over her mouth as he urges her toward the idling van in a few quick movements—enlisting Goldberg to help him push— no—lift Grace up and inside, then scrambling in after her and slamming the doors shut.

131.

"Death ends a life, not a relationship." —Jack Lemmon

John scurries around the base of the piñata tree—almost tripping on some hard candies still rolling on the cobblestones—then trots through the line of people outside the restaurant and into the street, searching for Grace.

But the van that has spirited Grace away is already moving fast down Alameda Street.

Does John have the sense—or the luck—necessary to actually do something right now that could possibly help Grace?

I can't wait to see what the hipster goateed fucking assistant will do when he realizes that she's gone.

"She's gone. They've taken her. Didn't you see?" I say to Hope. "Let's go."

Hope shakes her head, her copper hair tarnished now.

As she moves away from the altar, she's faded.

"I can't, Hope whispers—a pallid emanation now. "I'm sorry, Charles. Remember how much Grace loved you. Help her if you can."

Hope flickers and goes dark.

And Rose is ahead—floating over the van traveling fast toward La Moda Street.

I look back at the empty air where Hope just was, then plunge into the deepening night—following Rose and searching for Grace.

132.

"Life is but a mask worn on the face of death. And is death, then, but another mask?" —Joseph Campbell

Rose is above the van as it rocks around the corner to La Moda Street and I pass—grayish dead bare feet first—through the van's roof—to the interior.

Grace is alive.

The black and white greasepaint on her face is smudged gray in places—but her eyes are bright.

She sits cross-legged between Goldberg and the dwarf on the van's ridged metal floor among damaged Halloween piñatas, empty trash bags and cardboard boxes.

The dwarf wears his black skull mask pushed down around his neck—his thick muscled arm is a restraint around her slim shoulders—and he grips a small, black gun.

Goldberg muzzles Grace with one sunburned, black-fingernailed hand and holds her wrists together with the other.

"Grab hard," the dwarf tells Goldberg, "Don't let go."

The dwarf lets go of Grace, crawls to a thick roll of duct tape, crawls back, tears off a long piece, winds it around Grace's wrists and hands, then tears another piece and flattens it against Grace's mouth.

Goldberg watches—his lachrymal eyes Keane-dark and enormous—his weirdly feminine lips open, "Look, señor. I appreciate the job and all—but this is way more than I signed up for."

"Don't shit yourself, cobarde," the driver says. "Just shut the fuck up and do what he tells you."

Rose descends into the dim interior as the van bumps to a

274

stop—

When she sees Grace muzzled and restrained, the fur on Rose's neck rises and she bares her teeth.

Rose rushes to place herself between Grace and the dwarf—then turns toward him and releases a rough half-groan, half growl.

133.

"The real question of life after death isn't whether or not it exists, but even if it does what problem this really solves." — Ludwig Wittgenstein

The driver stops the van, hops out and disappears around the back.

I hear what sounds like a garbage truck roll past—and then a moment of quiet before the back doors creak open and the driver climbs inside.

"Wait—don't let go until I tell you," the dwarf tells Goldberg—then he nods at the driver, "Vamos a dar al piso de arriba."

The driver holds Grace with both hands while the dwarf pulls off his mask and pushes it over her face to cover the tape.

"Shitface. Put some stuff in the bag and carry it with you," the driver instructs Goldberg, glancing at the damaged piñatas on the floor, "and bring the tape."

Goldberg stuffs some of the piñatas in a bag, drops the fat roll of duct tape in the bag, and looks at the dwarf as if awaiting further orders.

The dwarf scuttles to standing position—but the taller driver and Grace remain hunched over—as they maneuver Grace out the back, down onto the curb and push her toward the metal shuttered door of Andreas's shop on La Moda street.

Goldberg—dutifully carrying the trash bag—is right behind them.

The night-muffled street—the small group of quiet people—make this look like a delivery, not a kidnapping, despite the ghost dog above the victim's head.

"Put down the bag," the dwarf tells Goldberg. "Now you hold her, too."

Goldberg drops the bag and places an arm around tightly Grace's shoulders. The driver is still restraining Grace as the dwarf bends down and unlocks the padlock, releases the security shutters, and rolls it upwards.

134.

"What happens after death is so unspeakably glorious that our imagination and our feelings do not suffice to form even an approximate conception of it." —Carl Jung

A few excruciatingly long seconds drag themselves painfully into oblivion during which interval no wandering drunk or late-night cyclist or police officer or guardian fucking angel appears to rescue the woman I love from her fate—

Not one good thing fucking happens on La Moda Street.

The van driver and the dwarf push Grace inside and Goldberg follows with the bag.

The dwarf closes the metal shutter from the inside, switches on the lights, then he and the driver shove Grace to the back, knocking down stuffed animals, hula hoops, and cheap backbacks, Halloween costumes and suitcases from the wall as they go.

"Over here," the dwarf calls Goldberg to the back near Grace. "Sostenla—hold her."

Goldberg relinquishes the bag and apologetically gazes into Grace's eyes behind the dwarf's black skull mask as he yanks Grace's arms out in front of her.

The dwarf fishes in the bag for the duct tape, rips off a long a piece and then another, and tapes Grace's ankles together, then fishes in her pants pocket and takes her cell phone.

"Now it's time to pay you," the dwarf says.

Goldberg brightens—or I should say—his shiny face darkens to an alarmingly liverish crimson.

The driver and the dwarf exchange a look—then the driver tackles Goldberg.

Goldberg tumbles onto the stained industrial carpeting, his

lungs releasing a loud huff of air.

The driver efficiently duct tapes Goldberg's sockless and freckled ankles tightly together—then secures his wrists behind his back—and silences his protests with two strips of tape across the mouth.

"Voy a llamar a Mateo y Andreas," the dwarf says goes to the front with his phone held near his face.

135.

"He is dying the death that everyone dies…" —Lawrence Ferlinghetti

Grace—still wearing the dwarf's skull mask—is on the floor, resting against the bookcase that hides the door to the second floor.

Rose has stationed herself above the reddish wig on Grace's head, alert, protective—her eyes on the store entrance.

Goldberg is in a semi-fetal position near Grace's feet—his ruby cheek pressed into the carpeting—his Gollum-eyes moist with fear or anger.

The only sounds are the captives' nasal inhalations and exhalations—and the ringing from the dwarf's cell phone—then a long beep and a male voice delivering a message in Spanish.

"Ven aca," the dwarf says, motioning the driver to the front of the shop.

A few more words in Spanish, then the rasp of the metal shutter being opened and closed—the clank of the padlock outside being locked again—and then the rumble of the van's engine.

Do I follow them or stay with Grace?

136.

"Of all ghosts the ghosts of our old loves are the worst."
—Arthur Conan Doyle

I stay close to Grace.

Her dark eyes behind the mask search the shop for a way out, then search again.

Grace sees something.

She leans to one side, drops sideways to the floor and rolls on her back—then lifts her legs, pushing off from the bookcase.

The bookcase rocks and crashes down and with it the plastic Halloween skulls, rubber rats and Styrofoam R.I.P. headstones that that occupied the shelves.

Slowly—still on her back and pushing with her feet—Grace propels herself a few feet away from where she started.

When Goldberg sees the door, he emits a strangled, high-pitched sound, then rolls onto his back—pinning his restrained hands.

After some moaning and snuffly breathing through his flaring nostrils, Goldberg rolls again—farting resoundingly and repeatedly—until he's finally face-down.

What the hell is he doing?

Grace rolls to her side and watches as Goldberg farts and grunts and flops and his way—not to the door—but away from it to a small, high table and stool in the corner.

Goldberg's face is scary now—blotched purple—glossy with sweat—his stringy hair sticking to his pink scalp—the lime green My Food Shits On Your Food t-shirt worked up into a roll under his armpits—his weirdly pale and hairless stomach contracting and expanding as he forces air into and out of his nostrils.

Grace begins to move—rolling over and over among and over the Halloween decorations she knocked down—toward Goldberg.

Grace and has an easier time than Goldberg because her hands are taped in front —and as she rolls, she succeeds in pushing the mask down around her neck—and smears off some of the face paint on the carpet.

When she's close to Goldberg, Grace stops—then struggles to sit up—but falls hard onto her side.

She rolls onto her back, scoots close to the table and tries again—and this time she stays upright.

Grace stares at Goldberg and then at the table.

Goldberg's eyes widen as Grace lifts her duct-taped hands up above her head and then brings them hard and fast on the metal table's corner—

I get it—Grace is trying to break the tape that's wrapped around her wrists—

Grace cries out in pain—the tape holds but the table topples over and with it the small cash register, a metal cash box, and glass vase holding an artificial rose that shatters against the wall.

Rose barks in alarm—then floats to the towel-covered cages now exposed to view.

Rose points her nose at the cages then stares at me and barks sharply.

Jesus.

The birds.

"I know, Rosie," I say. "I know."

Rose darts to Grace and back again to the cages in the corner.

Goldberg grunts and nods toward the wall.

Grace makes an incoherent sound, then scoots on her ass toward the broken glass until she's close enough to touch a nasty-looking shard with her taped-together fingertips.

Goldberg wiggles toward Grace, a huge, rumbling fart

escaping as he goes.

Grace tries to grasp the piece of glass with her fingertips—but she can't get a grip.

Grace sits then—her chest heaving for a few moments—and stares at her shoes.

They're boots, really—sharp-toed black leather ankle boots with low heels.

Grace bends and positions her taped wrists next to her right shoe—then works the tape against the toe of her boot until it loosens a little.

Grace keeps working—the smudged greasepaint making her face look like a vandalized Picasso—the wig half off now, her black curls bobbing front of her eyes.

Grace finally works the tape off her wrists—then starts over—forcing the tape around her hands down toward her fingertips.

137.

"And yonder all before us lie / Deserts of vast eternity."
—Andrew Marvell

After twenty minutes—maybe more—Grace wiggles her delicate fingers and her palms free of the tape.

She shakes the numbness from her hands, untapes her ankles, then liberates Goldberg from his restraints—letting him remove the tape from his own mouth.

"Ow," Goldberg says.

Grace closes her eyes and rips the tape off her lips, "Jesus. That hurts."

"You're quite salty," Goldberg says, his voice hoarse. "I'm Goldberg by the way."

"I'm Grace. And yeah, I'm salty," Grace says. "Now, Mr. Goldberg, how do we get the fuck out of here?"

Goldberg bends down and rubs his ankles, then squints and looks around the shop. "I have to tell you that I am uncomfortable with profanity. But I understand, Grace. We are in difficult situation."

"Jesus H. Christ," Grace says under her breath, then louder, "I'll check the front, you look around back here." Grace moves quickly to the front of the store and examines the locked shutter.

"There's no way to unlock the padlock outside," Grace says.

"Maybe there's something I can find to pick the lock in the door back here," Goldberg says, examining the lock. Then he is stepping through broken glass and Halloween items to the spot where the table stood in the corner, kneeling by the cash register and trying to open the drawer.

"Look for paper clips. Hangers."

Rose whines as Goldberg moves near the covered cages. "I can't open this darned drawer. Maybe there are some tools in these boxes." Goldberg pulls the pink towel off the top cage.

Rose yelps.

"Oh my goodness—what are these? Birds?"

138.

"I shut my eyes and all the world drops dead / I lift my eyes and all is born again." —Sylvia Plath

Rose circles the air above Goldberg and Grace.

They sit cross-legged on the carpet, removing the birds from the cardboard tubes and untaping their beaks until a dozen parrots—eyes shut—are lined up unmoving on the pink towel.

"They're dead." Grace says. "Suffocated maybe. We have to find a way out now. Shorty and his pal could be back any minute."

But Goldberg's soggy eyes bestow a dreamy look on the unmoving parrots. He lifts one with both red hands and tenderly presses its green breast to his ear.

"I hear a heartbeat, Grace." Goldberg tilts the bird toward Grace, "But I don't think its little lungs are working."

"Sad," Grace says. "I've heard they sell smuggled animals here on La Moda Street—" She gently touches the feathers on the parrot's unmoving breast with her finger. "This poor guy is why that's against the law. But we've got to focus our own problems."

But Goldberg—like Rose who has drifted down close to the bird—remains fixated on the parrot.

Goldberg gently, tilts the bird's head back, opens its beak, and covers its tiny nostrils with a thumb and forefinger.

Then he inflates his flaming cheeks and blows five small mouthfuls of air into the parrot's tiny mouth.

Jesus.

Goldberg lifts the bird so that its breast is level with his fog-colored eyes. "Rescue breathing, Grace. If that doesn't work we can do CPR."

139.

"Death is just the last scene of the last act." —Joyce Carol Oates

"They need water. And food," Goldberg says. "I think they've been drugged, don't you?"

Goldberg—and then Grace and Goldberg—have resuscitated six parrots.

"Makes sense," Grace says, desperate. "They're out of it. But if we want to do anything for them, we have to get out of here. Now."

"Okay." A sorrowful Goldberg lovingly returns the unconscious birds to the cage and covers the dead birds with the towel.

"You said you knew how to pick locks?" Grace says.

"I'm ashamed to admit it, but yes," Goldberg says. "Look for paperclips. Or a wire hanger. Or maybe a hook—a thin one, please, Grace."

Grace begins a wild search of the shop, tossing merchandise to the floor, knocking items down, baring shelves and inspecting the hardware.

Goldberg's search is more methodical—more sedate—more like a meditation or a contemplation than a desperate attempt to escape confinement.

Goldberg stands in one spot then turns slowly—sweeping the place with his vague gaze.

After one slow spin he steps to the parrot cage, drops to his knees and starts fiddling with the cage.

"Shit, Goldberg," Grace says. "Just stop with the birds and find a goddamn pick."

"Please, Grace," Goldberg says. "Do I use profanity when speaking with you?"

Grace—flummoxed—sighs and picks up a plastic bucket shaped like a jack o'lantern and points to its curved, thin wire handle. "Hey, what about this?"

"Please bring the bucket here," Goldberg says. "I'm trying to remove the cage latch—and then I'll bend it into a hook. That handle might work as a rake."

140.

"You have to learn to do everything, even to die." —
Gertrude Stein

Rose floats above the cage housing the living birds.

She's watchful. Subdued.

Goldberg—with raw fingers—succeeds in removing and straightening a length of wire from the latch as Grace removes the wire handle from the plastic bucket.

Goldberg sticks the end of the wire in his mouth, then bites down hard to shape one end into a hook. With his fingers he straightens the bucket wire. "One is the rake, Grace," he says, "the other is the hook."

"Great," Grace says, impatient. "Show me how they work."

Goldberg steps very close to the door, leans down, and presses the hooked wire into the lock, then turns it. "The hook turns the lock, applying tension."

"Yeah," Grace says, uncertain.

"Now," Goldberg inserts the straight wire into the opening, "I'm scraping the pins straight with the rake—"

Goldberg jiggles both wires for a few seconds, his face close to the lock.

Then there's a click.

141.

"Death is the greatest illusion of all." —Osha Rajneesh

Rose stays with the birds.

I float above the dark blur that is Grace climbing the stairs two by two—until the security door halts her progress.

"Shit," she says. "Another fucking door. Can you see, Goldberg?"

Goldberg is right behind her, but his ascent is slower. Maybe he's tired from the work he did rolling around and fabricating the picks. Maybe he's sick.

A faint glow from the shop downstairs and two greenish Halloween light sticks Grace holds aloft provide the only illumination.

Goldberg—like a blind person—examines the security door and the lock with his raw fingertips.

"I think I can pick this. But there's another door behind it."

"Try," Grace urges. "Please."

Goldberg nods, removes the wires from the pocket of his khakis, kneels, and inserts first one and then the other into the lock's opening.

It feels like forever until Goldberg opens the security door and gets to work on the interior lock.

142.

"Silence is death. If you speak, you die. If you are silent, you die. So speak, and die." —Taha Djaout

A soft click and Goldberg defeats the final lock.

Grace reaches to open the door when Goldberg stops her with his hand.

"How do we know it's empty?" Goldberg whispers.

"It's dark. It's quiet. No one came to the door when you were fiddling with the lock, right?" Grace says softly.

"That short man had a gun. I'm going first," Goldberg says, throwing the door open and—chin out—resolutely stepping into the dark space.

There's a deep hush—then sound like a bag of rocks being dropped—and a groan.

Grace runs inside and almost trips over Goldberg sprawled on the floor among piñatas, and black trash bags filled with shredded paper.

"Are you okay?"

"I'm fine," Goldberg says. "I tripped. Be careful, Grace. There's stuff all over the place. But don't turn on the lights," Goldberg warns, "someone outside might see us through that window."

Grace blinks, her eyes adjusting to the darkness, then turns toward the dim gray rectangle that is the window—feeling her way along the table, among the piñatas and bags of shredded paper.

Grace reaches the window and holds both light sticks close, then pops them in her mouth, turns the latch with both hands, and slides the window up and open.

A rush of night air carries with it the murmur of distant traffic and then—growing insistent—the shriek of sirens.

"Do you hear that?" Grace asks. "The police are on their way."

Goldberg leans out the window, looks down alley two floors below and then at the fire escape. "Hurry, Grace. We've got to get the birds."

143.

"In sorrow we must go, but not in despair. Behold! we are not bound for e'er to the circles of the world, and beyond them is more than memory." —J.R.R. Tolkien

Four black and white police cars skid into the alley behind La Moda Street.

Their headlights immerse Grace in their radiance.

Grace—holding her red wig and the two dying light sticks—her face still smeared in places with greasepaint—still wearing Hope's death clothes—but now wearing a backpack backwards so the pack covers the bloodstain on the front of her shirt—blinkingly waves them forward.

Despite Grace's assurances that she would help him—that the police would not arrest him—that she promised to befriend him—Goldberg is gone.

"People like you aren't friends with people like me," Goldberg had said, then gallantly shook Grace's pale white hand with his red one and loped down the alley and into the night.

If it weren't for Rose and me floating close, Grace would be alone.

The door of the black and white flies open and a slim, young female Hispanic officer carrying a huge flashlight trots toward Grace. "Are you all right, Miss?" she says. "What happened?"

"Long story, but I'm okay," Grace says, "But I need a vet right away."

Grace pats the backpack.

"I've got some birds that are in really bad shape."

144.

"You are a little soul carrying around a corpse." —Epictetus

The wet sidewalk reverse-mirrors the glowing red neon of THE LAST BOOK STORE sign in the window on South Spring Street.

A slender woman in black boots, black leggings and a black sweater shares an umbrella with a man in skinny jeans and a leather jacket.

The couple fits right in among the hipsters migrating to the bookstore after their ramen dinners at the Grand Central Market on Broadway—their murmured conversations mixing with the metallic sound of descending rain—they step lightly past the silent homeless who've retreated into narrow doorways.

The man holds the umbrella and his free hand encloses the woman's hand in his. As they turn the corner, the woman rests her head on the man's shoulder.

Rose watches them enter the spacious store—gives me a quizzical and impatient look—and then floats through the glass window to the store's interior.

I stay where am in the blue mist above the sidewalk—but it could be the last time I see Grace.

I travel through the glass and locate Grace and John in the columned, high-ceilinged space.

Rose hovers happily above them as they admire a Christmas tree constructed of books, then she ascends high above the bowed heads of the readers and browsers to the second floor.

"I forgot how much I love this place," Grace says. Her cheeks are flushed and a few raindrops sparkle like crystals in her hair.

"Me, too." John says. "It's awesome. Just like you."

Jesus.

Grace goes from flushed to full-on blushing.

What the fuck? Is she a teenager now?

"You're blushing," John says.

"I'm not," Grace says. "It's just the vegan ramen. I think it overheated me."

"I think you overheat me," John says, the tattoo on his neck contracting as he leans down and plants a very long kiss on Grace's mouth.

Shit. Really?

Grace gulps when the kiss is finally over and takes a breath. "I'm going upstairs to the Labyrinth. I want to look for that Agnes Martin book I saw here about six months ago and didn't buy. Before—everything—happened."

Grace becomes somber.

But John squeezes her lovely hand and her expression brightens.

"I'll bet it is still there," John says, squeezing her lovely hand. "Come on, I'll help you find it."

145.

"To practice death is to practice freedom…" —Montaigne

I stare past Rose into the borderless nothingness.

Rose sulks.

"Okay. I get it. They're a thing," I say. "Grace and John. John and Grace. Yeah. Maybe they'll elope. Isn't that enough?"

Rose replies by flipping on her back—legs up—paws up—tail slack.

"Grace is safe and happy. And that's all that matters."

Rose's tail swings once.

But I say nothing.

How do I explain to a dead dog that witnessing Grace's particular happiness lacerates me?

It's fucking unbearable.

Excruciating.

"I'm sorry I pulled you away from Grace," I say to Rose, scratching the soft, fine fur behind her ears. "But sometimes the best thing to do is to get the fuck out."

Rose turns her head, gives me a sideways look and curls up.

But for once I'm right, and Rose is—forgive me—dead wrong.

Not because of any fault in her, but because she's a dog.

There are things Rose will never understand—

That people like Grace can't love people like me.

That I never stopped loving Grace and never will.

That maybe that's enough.

Rose can't know that Andreas wasn't shipping Gordo Locos

drug cash to Mexico—just the opposite.

That he was funneling the drug money through California Dreaming—exchanging the cash for merchandise that he shipped to Mexico. Once the stuff sold in Mexico, the clean money went right to the cartel.

That Hope—while investigating wage theft at California Dreaming—either found out or poked around too much—and put herself and anyone connected to her in danger.

And so—to protect Grace—she killed herself.

That the police arrived at the alley behind the La Moda Street shop to rescue Grace—and the parrots—not because John the hipster assistant fucking mixologist life coach boyfriend grew a brain and called the cops when he couldn't find her—

No.

The cops showed up because Joshua and the valet from the pot shop had attempted a home invasion robbery at Andreas's house—

Andreas's wife called the police and they found drugs and $800,000 in cash in Andreas's office.

Andreas, Mateo, the dwarf, and the driver were arrested.

The schlock shop on La Moda Street, the bird smuggling operation, Fiesta Piñata's and California Dreaming were shut down.

Rose relaxes a little, her eyes forgiving and wise and kind.

Rose knows all she needs to know—

That life is sweet and cruel.

And that death—which brought me to her and her to me—is good.

146.

"…for I too must have lived, once, out there, and there is no recovering from that." —Samuel Beckett

Rose loves it here—loves the way the hills drop suddenly below the Colorado Street Bridge—loves the way a hawk hangs in the dry December air—then glides above the scrub and jumble of hillside houses like a ghost.

Rose doesn't know that the bridge is famous for its suicides.

Or that the building we approach from high above—the Ninth Circuit Court of Appeals—downtown in the hazy distance and the Pacific beyond—was once a hotel.

So what?

Rose goes straight for what matters—the tall palm trees in front.

The squawking and chattering gets brassier and more insistent as we approach.

Rose follows the noise up one palm's rough trunk almost to the crown—and discovers a small flock of parrots squabbling among the parrot-green fronds—their red-ringed eyes full of life.

Rose pauses to watch the birds—then rises with them as one pair suddenly flutters into flight—their uplifted wings strong, free and exultant in the empty sky.

The End.

About the author.

Jo Perry earned a Ph.D. in English, taught college literature and writing, produced and wrote episodic television, and has published articles, book reviews and poetry. She lives in Los Angeles with her husband, novelist Thomas Perry. They have two adult children. Their two cats and two dogs are rescues.

Also by Jo Perry and published by Fahrenheit Press

Dead Is Better

Dead Is Best

34715905R00178

Printed in Great Britain
by Amazon